TROUBLE ON THE TRAIL

Phil and his horse, Teddy, were off, trotting past a gathering of ferns and crossing a field. Phil was definitely trying to avoid Stevie.

"All I wanted to say," she yelled, "was—" But at this instant Teddy broke into a canter. Stevie could hear his hooves thud on the brown winter grass.

Abruptly there was a flash of white ahead. A fawn darted across the road in front of Teddy, its tail high.

Without warning Teddy reared, giving a whinny that sounded to Stevie like a scream. Phil's arms were around Teddy's neck, his knees high. Then, as Stevie watched in horror, Teddy lost his balance and fell with a thud. Phil flew off the horse and landed in the rocks beside the trail in an awkward position. . . .

THE S_____LUB

HIGH
HORSE

BONNIE BRYANT

A BANTAM SKYLARK BOOK®
NEW YORK • TORONTO • LONDON • SYDNEY • AUCKLAND

RL 5, 009–012

HIGH HORSE

A Bantam Skylark Book / April 1994

*Skylark Books is a registered trademark of Bantam Books,
a division of Bantam Doubleday Dell Publishing Group, Inc.
Registered in U.S. Patent and Trademark Office and elsewhere.*

*"The Saddle Club" is a trademark of Bonnie Bryant Hiller.
The Saddle Club design / logo, which consists of an inverted
U-shaped design, a riding crop, and a riding hat is a
trademark of Bantam Books.*

ISBN 0-553-48147-9

Published simultaneously in the United States and Canada

Bantam Books are published by Bantam Books, a division of Bantam
Doubleday Dell Publishing Group, Inc. Its trademark, consisting of the
words "Bantam Books" and the portrayal of a rooster, is Registered in
U.S. Patent and Trademark Office and in other countries. Marca Regis-
trada. Bantam Books, 1540 Broadway, New York, New York 10036.

PRINTED IN THE UNITED STATES OF AMERICA

CWO   0 9 8 7 6 5 4 3 2 1

I would like to express my special thanks to Helen Geraghty for her help in the writing of this book.

"ONLY NINE CLAWS," Stevie Lake muttered to her best friends, Lisa Atwood and Carole Hanson. "She's practically defenseless."

Veronica diAngelo was standing in the center of the ring at Pine Hollow Stables, holding her right hand so she could look at the fingernail she'd just broken. It was a clean break, so now she had nine sharp red nails and one stump.

"You poor *thing*," Betsy Cavanaugh said to Veronica.

Carole rolled her eyes, and Stevie looked to see if Betsy was kidding, but she wasn't. Betsy's face was screwed up into an expression of sympathetic woe,

1

making Stevie realize that there were some members of Horse Wise who would do anything to get in good with snooty Veronica, even cry over her broken fingernail.

"Maybe you could get it wrapped," Polly Giacomin said.

Stevie groaned. Then she immediately realized that she'd groaned louder than she should have, because all the riders in the ring were now staring at her.

"Of course some people have no nails to lose," Veronica said, looking at Stevie's short nails.

The next thing Stevie knew, everyone was staring at her fingernails. Stevie felt her face turn pink. She had no desire to have long fingernails. There was no way she could groom Topside or keep his tack clean if she was worrying about her nails. But still, right this minute, she wouldn't mind having two-inch-long claws so she could—

"Horse Wise, come to order," Max Regnery said, interrupting Stevie's thoughts. Horse Wise was a Pony Club that met Saturday mornings at Pine Hollow Stables to learn everything there was to know about horses. This morning Veronica and Peter Allman were going to give a Big Sister / Little Brother demonstration of the fine points of horse grooming.

Max Regnery was the owner of Pine Hollow Stables

and the head of Horse Wise. Right now, after listening to Veronica go on about her fingernails, his blue eyes were twinkling. Stevie realized that it was no accident he had assigned Veronica the subject of horse grooming. Max was expecting this to be an interesting morning.

"In a minute Veronica and Peter are going to give a grooming demonstration," Max said. "But first, there's bad news."

The members of Horse Wise groaned.

"We may not be able to go on the Mountain Trail Overnight," Max said.

The three members of The Saddle Club exchanged worried glances. This *was* bad news. Last year's MTO, or Mountain Trail Overnight, had been absolutely wonderful. Their days had been filled with riding along the beautiful trails in the mountains of Virginia. At night they had slept out in the woods under the stars, and in the morning Max had prepared Max's Morning Madness, a special breakfast feast. Everything about the MTO had been perfect, and the Saddle Club girls were expecting this year's to be just as thrilling, perhaps even better.

Carole noticed that two of the younger riders, Jackie and Amie, looked as if they were about to cry.

This was going to be their first MTO, and they had been looking forward to it for months.

"Adam Levine has a strep throat," Max went on. "As you know, we were counting on Adam to help load the horses into the vans and supervise the temporary paddock. We can't go on the MTO unless we can find an experienced rider to replace him."

"The rest of us could work extra hard," Carole chimed in quickly. Lisa and Stevie quickly assented with nods. After all, they had originally formed The Saddle Club because they were totally horse crazy. They were willing to work all day and night if that's what it took to go on the MTO.

But Max shook his head. "That's a help," he said, "but we really need an experienced rider."

"Hmmmm," Stevie said, running her hand under Topside's mane and scratching him in a spot he particularly liked.

"Get ready," Lisa warned the others. Stevie was notorious for coming up with ideas that were bombshells.

"This is possibly the best idea anyone ever had," Stevie said.

Lisa and Carole exchanged smiles, because Stevie always thought her ideas were brilliant.

"Anyone with a suggestion can talk to me after

class," Max said. "Right now Veronica and Peter will give their demonstration."

"Peter," Veronica demanded. "Where are you?"

Peter Allman stepped forward. He wasn't the youngest member of Horse Wise—Amie and Jackie were six, a year younger—but he was the shortest and, at the moment, the most miserable. As Veronica spoke, his ears turned bright pink. Stevie wondered why Max had assigned this poor, defenseless kid to be Veronica's younger brother. But then, Max had his mysterious ways, and he never did anything without a plan.

"First, we'll tether Garnet," Veronica said in a loud voice. She gestured at her Arabian, who stood patiently waiting for her grooming. Garnet was a beautiful horse, alert, with a small head and big dark eyes. In The Saddle Club's opinion, Veronica didn't appreciate Garnet nearly as much as the horse deserved.

"Please tether Garnet, Peter," Veronica commanded.

Peter's ears got even redder, but he took the lead rope and tied it to a post in the paddock fence.

"Aren't we forgetting something, Peter?" Veronica said.

"She didn't give the poor kid a chance," Stevie murmured.

Peter reached into the grooming-kit bucket and

pulled out another lead rope. He clipped one end to the opposite side of Garnet's halter and then tied the other end of the rope to a post.

"Does anyone know why we use a double tether?" Veronica asked.

Peter opened his mouth, about to answer, but before he could get the words out, Betsy Cavanaugh said, "For extra security. So the horse can't drift."

"Very good, Betsy," Veronica said. "And now for the next step. Peter, get the dandy brush." Peter picked the largest brush from the kit bucket.

"I suppose you can reach Garnet's fetlocks, Peter," Veronica said in a voice dripping with sarcasm.

Peter turned even redder, because this was a reminder of how short he was. He put his left hand on Garnet's shoulder to warn her that he was about to touch her leg. Then he leaned down and brushed Garnet's right front hoof and leg with the dandy brush.

"Very good, Peter," Veronica said. "Now you can do the same with Garnet's other three legs."

"Like Peter doesn't know how many legs a horse has," Lisa said. She couldn't help it. Veronica was being such a pain. When Amie and Jackie heard her remark, they fell into a fit of giggles.

Peter cleaned Garnet's left rear leg and moved to

the other side of the horse, so that now only Peter's legs and feet could be seen.

"I don't mind the Big Sister/Little Brother program," Veronica said, looking at Peter's skinny legs on the other side of Garnet, "but do little brothers have to be so *little?*"

This time Betsy Cavanaugh and Polly Giacomin broke up, as if this were the wittiest thing that anyone had ever said.

Peter came out from behind Garnet and put the brush into the bucket.

"Body brush and currycomb," Veronica said.

Peter pulled a smaller brush and a currycomb from the pail and handed the brush to Veronica.

"Why do we use the body brush?" Veronica asked, sounding more like a teacher than a thirteen-year-old girl.

"To get rid of scurf," Betsy said.

"Very good, Betsy," Veronica said. "And, for our younger riders, what is scurf?"

"Horse dandruff," Betsy said.

"And why would we want to get rid of horse dandruff?"

Stevie couldn't resist.

"So the horses can get more dates," she said. Amie and Jackie exploded with laughter.

"Stevie," Max warned.

Veronica shot Stevie a nasty look.

"I will now use the body brush," she announced imperiously.

It's a first! Stevie wanted to say, but she bit her tongue.

Veronica ran the brush down Garnet's gleaming chestnut neck, but almost at once there was trouble. Veronica stopped, muttering to herself and fussing with her fingernails.

"Now we see why serious riders don't have long fingernails," Carole whispered. The long red nails of Veronica's left hand were snagged in Garnet's mane.

Veronica worked her nails loose and handed the body brush to Peter, who cleaned it with the curry-comb.

"Water brush," Veronica snapped. Peter handed her a small, damp brush and she went to work on Garnet's mane.

A few minutes later she handed it back to the boy.

"Peter, brush the tail," she said.

"You don't catch Veronica diAngelo doing tails," Carole commented.

"Oh dear no," Lisa said. "Too vulgar."

Max glanced over at the girls, deliberately placing a finger over his lips.

Peter let the dark chestnut hair of Garnet's tail fall through his fingers as he brushed it. Garnet nodded her head and nickered with pleasure. The horse was definitely wasted on Veronica.

While Peter finished grooming Garnet, Stevie watched impatiently. Usually she loved Pony Club meetings, especially the mounted ones, but she couldn't wait for today's to be over. She was dying to tell her friends the wonderful idea she'd come up with to save the MTO. She'd decided to ask Max if her boyfriend Phil Marsten could come along. Phil was a member of another Pony Club called Cross County. Recently he had been with Pony Wise on a mock hunt, and Max knew that he was a skilled and experienced rider. It was perfect, Stevie mused. Max would get another rider; and she and Phil would have a great time.

Suddenly Stevie's head was filled with pictures of her and Phil on the MTO. They were riding side by side at dawn in a windswept meadow. Stevie could smell the wet earth, feel a cool mountain breeze. . . . She closed her eyes.

"Stevie!" It was Max. "How do you evaluate this demonstration? Is something missing?"

"Unh," Stevie said, blinking. "Veronica's fingernail?"

A few riders tittered, but this time Max was really annoyed. "Does anybody know?" He turned to Peter. "Do you?"

Peter's face turned redder, but he nodded.

"What?"

"We didn't pick Garnet's hooves," Peter said in a voice so soft that it was hard to hear. "We should have started with the hoof pick."

In spite of Max's annoyance at her for missing the answer, Stevie grinned. Veronica had been barking orders so fast that she hadn't given Peter a chance to make a single suggestion. Peter must have realized from the start that Veronica was making a mistake, but he'd been afraid to tell her. Stevie loved it—the little brother was showing up the big sister.

"That's right," Max said, giving the young rider an encouraging nod. "The first step in grooming is to clean your horse's hooves. A pebble caught between shoe and hoof can cause serious injury." Veronica's face turned beet-red. Not too long ago she hadn't been able to ride Garnet for two weeks for this very reason. She'd neglected to clean her horse's hooves properly.

Max turned to Veronica. "Teamwork goes both ways. Peter knew you'd forgotten the hoof pick, but you didn't give him a chance to say so. Now that we've got the Big Sister/Little Brother demonstrations underway, I'm going to start rating each one."

Lisa remembered back to the first demonstration. She had been a big sister to May, one of the younger riders. The demonstration had been a disaster because Lisa had been so bossy. She was glad Max hadn't rated it.

"I'm going to give this Big Sister/Little Brother team a rating of two out of a possible five, which means it needs improvement," Max said.

Stevie sighed with pleasure—not that she wished any harm to Peter. But on the other hand—

"And Stevie Lake's listening gets a rating of minus one out of a possible five."

Stevie felt herself flush. Max was joking, but he'd made his point.

"Thanks a lot," Veronica said, looking at Peter as if the whole thing were his fault.

"Veronica, you just learned something important," Max said. "In Big Sister/Little Brother projects both members of the team are equally important."

Veronica looked as if she thought this was complete nonsense. Peter, on the other hand, took a deep breath and stood up straight.

"Horse Wise dismissed," Max said.

Stevie headed straight for Max.

11

"I think I've got someone for the MTO," she said eagerly. "What about Phil Marsten? He's an experienced rider. He's good at loading horses. And he knows Silverado State Park because he lives near there."

"Phil would be fine," Max said, looking pleased. "I was impressed with him on the hunt. The only thing is, I have to know definitely whether he can come."

"Believe me, Phil will be on the MTO," Stevie quickly reassured him. If she knew Phil, there was no way he'd turn down the chance to ride for two days in the glorious mountains of Virginia.

Max grinned, his weathered skin crinkling. "When you say it that way, Stevie, I know it will happen."

Things are looking good, Stevie thought, as she started to lead Topside, the horse she always rode, back to the stable.

"Hey, Stevie."

She jumped. It was Joe Novick. With his curly brown hair and dark brown eyes, Joe was universally regarded as the cutest male member of Horse Wise. Amie and Jackie had crushes on him. Veronica and her friends were always inviting him to parties. And the three girls in The Saddle Club thought he was a really nice guy and wondered why he didn't have a girlfriend.

"I was thinking," Joe began when he caught up to her. "I can help on the MTO. I know I'm not an expert, but maybe you could give me some pointers about the things I don't know a lot about."

"You're doing great," Stevie reassured him. "You don't need my help."

Joe shook his head. "Would you believe I don't know how to pick hooves? I was standing there saying to myself that Peter Allman knows how to pick hooves and I don't."

"No problem!" Stevie said.

Joe broke into a grin. Joe was always handsome, but when he grinned, he was *really* handsome. "Then, you'll show me?"

"Better," Stevie said. "Next weekend you're going to have the opportunity of sharing a tent with one of the world's great riders. You remember Phil Marsten from the mock fox hunt?"

For some reason Joe didn't look as pleased as she'd expected. "Yeah," he said. "I remember him."

"He can teach you all kinds of things," Stevie went on eagerly. "He's a great hoof picker."

"I can hardly wait," Joe commented drily. "Can't you—"

"See you later, Joe," Stevie interrupted, suddenly catching sight of Lisa and Carole leading their horses,

13

Comanche and Starlight, inside the stable. "Hey, wait up, you guys! I have some fabulous news." She took off after her friends.

When Stevie reached Carole and Lisa, Carole gestured toward the spot where Stevie and Joe had been standing. "What was that?" she asked. "Has Handsome Joe finally gotten interested in a girl?"

Stevie laughed. "You're way off, Carole. He wants me to help him learn to pick hooves."

"Oh, right." Carole giggled.

Then, as Stevie filled them in on her plan to invite Phil on the MTO, Carole and Lisa exchanged looks. It was pretty obvious that Joe had a crush on Stevie.

STEVIE WAITED UNTIL all three of her brothers were out of sight. When her younger brother Michael had finally retreated to his bedroom to fuss with his guppies, and Alex, her twin, had gone over to his best friend Ron's house, and Chad, her older brother, had left for TD's, the local ice-cream parlor, with his current heartthrob, she sprang into action.

Stevie picked up the phone from the table where it stood in the hall and carried it into her room. Then, as a precaution that was frequently necessary in a household of brothers, she put a chair under the door-knob so no one could enter. Finally she dragged the phone into her closet and left the door open a crack to give herself enough light to enter the number. She had something important to talk to Phil about, and she was taking absolutely no chances.

Phil and Stevie had been dating ever since they'd met last summer at riding camp. She got to see him only a few times a month, but whenever they got together, they had a great time. The two of them not only had their love of horses and riding in common, they each had a great sense of humor. In fact that was one of the things Stevie liked best about Phil.

At the Marstens' house Phil's father answered. "Hi, Stevie," he said. "How's my favorite fox?"

Stevie had been the fox in the mock hunt that had been held by Horse Wise and Phil's Pony Club, and everyone still teased her about it. She had been an outstanding fox—perhaps the greatest human fox in history—but she was tired of being reminded of it. For months after the mock hunt Veronica and her friends had made jokes about Stevie's bushy tail and pointy ears.

"Fine," Stevie said briefly, wanting to give Mr. Marsten a gentle hint that she was tired of hearing about it.

Mr. Marsten seemed to get it. "I'll go get Phil," he replied hastily.

While she waited for Phil to come to the phone,

Stevie sat up straight, practicing her riding seat, something she did whenever she had an available moment. The secret was to be erect, but not stiff; firm, but flexible. Except, she thought, how can you be firm but flexible when you're sitting on a pile of shoes?

"Hey, Stevie," Phil said in his deep voice.

"Hi, Phil," Stevie said. "How's Teddy?" Teddy was Phil's horse.

"Teddy's excellent," Phil said. "Never better. And I'm sure he'll be touched to know you phoned to ask about him."

"Tell him Topside says hello," Stevie said.

"Sure," Phil agreed. Then he added, "Does Topside have a message for Teddy? I mean, is there something going on?"

"Could be," Stevie said.

"Teddy and I are all ears," Phil said.

Stevie giggled because Teddy was a fine-looking horse, but he did have big ears. When Phil leaned over his neck and talked to him, Teddy's ears stuck straight up like TV antennas.

"Topside has got this severe problem," Stevie said. "His eyes are kind of dull and he picks at his food. He keeps looking out the window of his stall and sighing."

"Sounds like love," Phil said.

"Spring fever," Stevie said. "A definite case of spring fever."

"Teddy and I can relate to that," Phil commented.

"Well, you know," she went on. "There's only one cure for spring fever."

"What's that?"

"A Mountain Trail Overnight. One of the boys can't come, and Max said we'd have to cancel the whole thing unless he could get another experienced rider. I told him you should come. He thought that was a great idea."

"Hmmmm," Phil said. "Sounds good to me, but . . ." His voice trailed off.

Stevie closed her eyes. Oh no, she thought. Phil can't come. What am I going to tell Max? What will everyone in Horse Wise say when they find out he can't go?

"Teddy was thinking more along the lines of the Bahamas," Phil went on in a very serious tone.

Relief washed over Stevie. Phil had just been joking! "Promise to take him there next year," Stevie joked. "This year he's coming on the MTO."

"I think I can convince him," Phil replied.

"There actually is a problem," Stevie said.

"I knew it." Phil sighed.

"You'll have to make a giant sacrifice."

"Be polite to Veronica?"

"Almost that bad," Stevie said. "It's a long week-end, so there won't be school on Monday, but you'll have to miss school on Tuesday."

"For you I'd miss school on Tuesday," Phil said. "And Wednesday. Possibly even Thursday."

"Gee, thanks, Phil. That's so generous," she replied.

"So who else is coming?" Phil asked. He knew most of the Horse Wise members from the mock hunt.

"The members of The Saddle Club, of course, in-cluding you," Stevie quickly added. Although she, Lisa, and Carole were the main members of the club, there were a few out-of-town members as well, and Phil was one of them.

"Right," he replied.

"Veronica diAngelo, of course," Stevie went on.

"Ugh. Who else?"

"Polly Giacomin."

"So many good-looking girls," Phil commented. "What about Betsy Cavanaugh?"

Alarm bells went off in Stevie's head. Betsy Cava-naugh had come to Carole's birthday party not long ago with James Spencer, but she had also been eyeing every available boy. If The Saddle Club was horse crazy, Betsy Cavanaugh was boy crazy. Actually, Betsy Cavanaugh wasn't boy crazy, she was boy *insane*. In fact she ran through boyfriends the way other people ran through breath mints. She had broken the heart of Stevie's brother Chad *twice*. Stevie hoped Betsy wouldn't flirt with Phil on the trip.

"Betsy's coming," Stevie said finally.

"It should be a good overnight," Phil said. "What about the guys?"

"Liam and Peter, who are kids. And Red O'Malley, the head stable hand, plus Max Regnery and Joe Novick."

"Joe Novick," Phil said. "Help me. What does he look like?"

"Curly dark-brown hair, brown eyes, not bad looking. You met him on the mock fox hunt."

"Not bad looking, huh?" said Phil. "Do I sense some competition here?"

"No way," Stevie replied. "He's a nice guy, but I'm not interested. Anyway, you'll have the chance to get to know him since you'll be sharing a tent with him."

"Fantastic," Phil said, sounding distinctly unenthusiastic to Stevie. "Any other surprises?"

"Max says we should wear our oldest riding clothes because the weather may be rough."

"No problem," Phil said. "Old riding clothes are all I have." The Marstens prided themselves on wearing well-aged riding gear. It was a family thing.

"Bring a rain jacket, rain pants, and rubber boots, just in case."

"Hmmmm," Phil said thoughtfully. "We might have to huddle together under a tree. Or maybe in an abandoned house. I like it already."

THE NEXT MORNING, as Stevie walked to Pine Hollow, she could smell wet leaves and pine needles. It would smell just like this along the trails on the MTO. She couldn't wait.

The Saddle Club was due to meet in ten minutes, and Stevie had lots of news. She hurried up the driveway.

Inside the stable Carole was mucking out a stall.

"It's impossible to get here before you," Stevie said. "Sometimes I think you sleep here."

"My dad dropped me on the way to the base," Carole said. Her father was a colonel in the Marine Corps, and he often worked on weekends, even Sundays.

The stall next to the one that Carole was mucking out belonged to Nero. Right now it was empty, probably because he was out in the paddock with a rider. Stevie took a pitchfork and speared some straw.

It was a rule at Pine Hollow that all riders had to help with chores to keep expenses down. Some riders

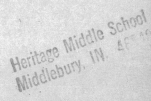

helped more than others, and Veronica never helped at all. But the members of The Saddle Club almost always wanted to help, because part of being horse crazy was caring about horses *all* the time, not just when they were doing the fun things, like riding them.

"So Phil's definitely coming on the MTO," Stevie said.

"Great!" Carole exclaimed. "You must be thrilled."

Stevie hesitated. The truth was, she'd never in her life looked forward to anything as much as this trip. But for some reason Phil's question about Betsy was haunting her. Why had he seemed so interested in Betsy? She started to tell Carole, then changed her mind. Stop it, Stevie, she told herself. You're getting worked up over nothing. She carried the clod of hay to the wheelbarrow. "I can't wait," she told her friend firmly. "It'll be a great time."

"Hi." It was Lisa. "You're early," she remarked to Stevie.

Stevie hadn't realized it, but Lisa was right. She'd actually gotten here an hour before they were supposed to meet. In fact Stevie had been looking forward to this meeting of The Saddle Club so much that she had gotten dressed and left the house in record time.

"Give me a hand," she said to Lisa. "As soon as we're done, we can start the meeting."

They worked silently, filling the wheelbarrow with forkfuls of straw. When they were finished, Lisa wheeled the straw toward the manure pile on the far side of the riding ring, and Stevie went to the feed room to get fresh straw, while Carole filled Nero's water bucket.

Finally they'd finished the chores and were ready for the best part of the day. Eagerly they settled into the clean straw in Nero's stall to begin their meeting.

"Phil's coming," Stevie told Lisa.

"Of course he is," Lisa said, matter-of-factly. "Who could turn down a chance to go on the MTO?"

"It's so romantic." Carole sighed as she leaned back in the straw. "You'll roast hot dogs together . . . you'll go for long walks. . . ."

"Ha!" came a voice from the next stall.

Veronica diAngelo stepped into view, wearing a new hacking jacket and a pair of breeches that looked as if they'd been custom-made. Veronica always seemed to be poking around Saddle Club meetings.

"How's your nail, Veronica?" Stevie asked drily. "Did you spend the night in the intensive-care unit of the nail hospital?"

Veronica held up her hands, showing ten perfect,

glossy red nails. "The nail is just like new. You'd never know anything had happened."

"I faint with relief," Stevie said.

Veronica tilted her head, letting her long, silky hair fall across her shoulder, and folded her arms across her chest. She gave Stevie a look of fake pity. "I'd be worried if I were you. Phil's going on the MTO—an overnight trip with almost all girls." She moved her hands so that her nails sparkled and then looked at Stevie's short nails and at her blond hair, which was a mess after doing all the chores. "The MTO is still almost a week away, Stevie. You still have time for a beauty makeover."

Stevie felt her face turn red. "What you need is a personality makeover, Veronica," she snapped.

"We'll see," Veronica said, smiling. "Personally, I think this MTO will be the best ever. Full of surprises." With that she turned to leave.

The Saddle Club sat there, looking at the empty spot where Veronica had been.

Then Stevie said, "Horse Wise does have a lot of good-looking girls. Phil happened to mention it."

"What did he say?" Lisa asked, looking surprised.

"You know—he can't wait, he'll be blinded by our beauty—stuff like that."

Carole grinned. "You have to admit, Horse Wise is dazzling."

"Especially the horses," Stevie joked. "Now if only we could figure out a way for horses to wear nail polish."

"Hoof polish," Carole said. "Hmmmm."

"Passion pink, petunia purple. I think we're on to a hot idea here," Stevie said.

"I'll be recording it," Lisa said. "The MTO that is."

Carole and Stevie looked puzzled.

"It's a school assignment," she explained. "Mr. Haegle, my English teacher, said the only way he would give me permission to miss school on Tuesday was if I kept a journal. We're reading *To Kill a Mockingbird* in class and studying the characters."

Carole and Stevie groaned simultaneously. The last time Lisa had written about horses, she wrote a theme for her English class about Pepper, a horse from Pine Hollow who had recently been put down. That had been great. But the time before, Lisa had written a column in *The Willow Creek Gazette*, which revealed all the shortcomings of Pine Hollow riders. Some riders were still angry about that one.

"Yuk," Stevie said. "Personally, I'd rather keep a tarantula than a journal."

"I only have to write two hundred fifty words a

day," Lisa said, "and I'm supposed to work on characterization."

"Well, there will be plenty of characters on this trip," Stevie said, thinking of Veronica.

"I'll be busy, too," Carole said. "Max has given me a Big Sister/Little Sister project. I'm going to be looking after Jackie and Amie, helping them tack up their horses and stow their gear. I probably won't be riding as much with you two."

"I might be busy, too." Stevie had a gleam in her eye.

"Really?" Carole said, elbowing her friend. "It wouldn't have anything to do with Phil's coming along—would it?"

"Now, Carole," Stevie replied innocently. "What on earth would give you that idea?"

HORSES WERE NEIGHING and pawing the ground. Riders were frantically checking supplies. The youngest riders were running back and forth like overexcited puppies.

Stevie knew the pandemonium was normal. Trips always seemed to start this way. At the moment it looked as if Horse Wise would spend the entire weekend at Pine Hollow trying to get organized.

The Marstens' horse van pulled into the parking lot. It wasn't a fancy van—Phil liked to joke that it had four colors: red, white, rust, and mud. But Stevie was glad to see it. She walked over to the driver's side.

"Hello, Stevie," Mr. Marsten said. "Ready for the overnight?"

Stevie nodded. "Yup. My horse is loaded; my gear is stowed; and I'm ready to go."

Phil got out of the passenger side, looked at the confusion, and said, "My Pony Club is the same way. We always get off to chaotic starts."

"Isn't it exciting?" exclaimed Stevie. "I can't wait to get started."

Phil gave her a warm smile. "Me either," he agreed. Then he went around to the back of the van, let down the ramp, and eased Teddy along it. Stevie was impressed. Horses never like walking backward, especially into a crowded scene like this one, but Phil kept Teddy calm by talking to him in a low voice.

Then Max came over and told Phil that as long as Teddy was calm, he might as well lead him directly into one of the vans that would take the horses to Silverado State Park.

Talking softly to Teddy, Phil led him into the van.

When Phil came out, Stevie said, "What were you saying to him? He looked so interested."

Phil's green eyes were shining. "Just making conversation."

"Horses can't understand English," Stevie said. "Max is always telling us that."

Phil grinned. "Who says we were talking English?"

Stevie was about to ask what language they were talking when Max came over and asked Phil to help Peter Allman sort out his tack, which had become tangled.

Phil obliged, and Stevie looked around. Nearly all the horses had been loaded, and most of the gear was stowed. Soon the riders would be taking off.

"Stevie," called a nearby voice. It was Joe Novick, standing patiently with his horse Rusty. Rusty's left front hoof was cocked forward slightly, a sign that he might have a rock stuck in his shoe.

"I think he has a stone," Joe said, "but I don't want to hurt him. Do you have a minute to give me a hand?" He held out a hoof pick.

"Sure," Stevie replied. She took the pick and went over to Rusty and put her hand on the horse's neck. "This isn't going to hurt." Rusty snorted and shook his head, but he let her touch him. Slowly she ran her hand down his shoulder and along his leg. When she reached his fetlock, she tapped it as a sign that he should raise his foot. Rusty nickered.

"We're going to get the stone out, and you'll have a great MTO," she said. Joe stood close to her, peering at Rusty's hoof.

"Now," she said, gently lifting Rusty's hoof with her

left hand. This was the moment when a horse could panic. "We're going to put the hook in here," Stevie said to Rusty. "Very gently."

Stevie turned to Joe. "A horse who's having his hooves picked is a lot like a human being at the dentist. He's nervous to begin with. Plus he's five times bigger than we are. Think of it as like being a little dentist with a very nervous five-hundred-pound customer."

"I would be careful," Joe said. "Real careful."

Stevie nodded. "Exactly." She ran the pick between Rusty's hoof and the shoe, looking for a lump.

"How will you know when you've hit it?" Joe asked.

"When the pick sticks. You have to be extra careful, because that's where Rusty's foot is sore. I think I feel something." She wiggled the pick gently—this was her favorite part of hoof picking. It took real artistry. "You can't force it, because the inside of a horse's hoof is sensitive. The outside is tough, like a fingernail, but the inside is as sensitive as the skin beneath a nail."

"You really know a lot," Joe said.

"It's coming." Suddenly the stone popped into the center of the shoe and bounced against the fleshy vee at the back of Rusty's hoof. Stevie picked up the stone, then slowly released Rusty's foot. "See," she said, showing it to Rusty. The stone was about the size of a pea. Rusty snorted and looked away.

"I guess it's yours," she said, dropping the stone into Joe's palm.

"That's the first thing you ever gave me," Joe said with a grin as he closed his fingers around the stone.

At that moment Stevie happened to see Phil over Joe's shoulder. Phil was giving her the strangest look. What's up with him? Stevie wondered.

AFTER COMANCHE HAD been boarded, and her gear shoved onto the van, Lisa perched on the top rail of the fence. She looked at the busy scene before her. Stevie was helping Joe Novick pick Rusty's hoof, and she looked totally engrossed in the task.

Phil was also watching Stevie, and he had a dark expression on his face. He's jealous, Lisa realized. How funny. . . . Stevie was worried about Phil's being interested in Betsy, while here he was, about to explode because Stevie was standing so close to Joe.

This is a perfect thing to write about in my journal, she thought. Then she reached into her pocket and pulled out the small notebook and pen she'd brought along for exactly this purpose.

* * *

31

"Okay," Carole said to Amie and Jackie, "what's the most important thing to remember about loading a horse into a van?"

Amie rolled her eyes. "You can't use force."

"Right," Carole said. "Why?"

Jackie was bouncing up and down on her heels with excitement at knowing the answer. "Because the next time that horse sees a van, he will totally and completely panic. You may never get him close to a van again."

"Exactly," Carole said. "What do you call that?"

Amie and Jackie both made faces, trying to think of the word.

"Imprinting," Carole said. "Like imprinting something on a page. If you force a horse into a van, you imprint him with van fear."

"Oh, yeah," Amie said. "I knew that."

Next Carole untied Patch, who was tethered to the paddock fence. Patch was one of the gentlest horses at Pine Hollow. He was a perfect choice to demonstrate loading. "Now you guys tell me what to do."

"Talk to him softly," Jackie said. "Like, pretend you're in love with him."

"Whisper mushy stuff to him," chimed in Amie.

The two girls giggled, but Carole shook her head.

"Get serious. Now tell me in detail. And no jokes either—"

Jackie and Amie exchanged grim looks.

From her perch on top of the white fence Lisa could see that Jackie and Amie were wondering if this overnight was going to be as much fun as they had thought. Sometimes Carole could be just too serious. But this was another good opportunity for Lisa. Mr. Haegle had said that the key to developing sympathetic characters was presenting their defects as well as their virtues. He had said, "Hint—keep an eye out for those characteristic faults." Whenever Mr. Haegle said "hint" he was telling his students what it took to get an A. Lisa always paid special attention to those hints.

Carole led Patch easily up the ramp and disappeared inside. While she was gone, Jackie punched Amie on the elbow, and Amie began chasing Jackie. As Lisa watched them play tag, she smiled. Poor Carole, she thought. She's trying to impart some horse wisdom to these two, and they're not in the least bit interested.

As Carole came out of the horse van, she took a deep breath, as if she were trying to quell her annoyance, and then looked around for the girls. By this time they were over at the other end of the paddock. Carole shook her head.

Just then Stevie came around the side of one of the horse vans, swinging her arms. Suddenly she got an evil look on her face. No, it wasn't evil, Lisa decided, that was going too far. Mr. Haegle had said that it was important not to exaggerate. Instead Stevie's expression was . . . devilish. Lisa saw that Stevie was looking at Veronica diAngelo, who had Red O'Malley, the head stable hand, checking her equipment list.

"Bringing your manicure set?" Stevie said with a nasty grin.

"I see you never got that beauty makeover," Veronica retorted. "What a shame."

"Cool it, girls," Red O'Malley said.

Another interesting situation. Lisa quickly started scribbling in her notebook. She couldn't believe how many fast-breaking stories there were on this MTO.

STEVIE WALKED AWAY from Veronica. There was no point in bothering with her. It was a pity Veronica was coming along on this MTO, but Stevie decided just to ignore her. Besides, it was time to find Phil and make sure that she got a seat next to him in the van. It was a two-hour drive to Silverado State Park. They could talk. They could joke.

But then she saw Phil helping Betsy Cavanaugh tie her sleeping bag. Gosh, Stevie thought, I knew Betsy was dumb, but can't she even tie a knot by herself?

"Phil, you got the sleeping bag so *flat!*" Betsy said admiringly.

Stevie waited for Phil to laugh at the ridiculous comment, but instead he smiled at Betsy and said, "It's something I learned out West. When you're strapping your bedroll behind your saddle, you want it to be really secure."

Stevie knew that this was true, and she knew that it's not easy to get your sleeping bag as compact as cowboys do. She had wrestled with this problem when she was staying at The Bar None Dude Ranch, and the truth was that she had never gotten her bag as flat as she would have liked it. But there was no reason for Phil and Betsy to worry about compact sleeping bags right now. Betsy's bag would simply be stowed in the bus along with everyone else's. Who cares if it's bulky, Stevie thought.

"Which do you like best?" Betsy breathed. "Western saddles or English?"

Stevie couldn't believe that Phil was paying attention to such a dumb question. You couldn't compare Western and English saddles. They were like apples and oranges.

"They have different purposes," Phil said. "A Western saddle is geared for all-day comfort and for roping and tying calves. An English saddle is designed for precision and speed."

"I guess you're really good at both kinds of riding," Betsy said.

Stevie couldn't take any more. This is the dumbest conversation I've ever heard, she thought, and marched on by.

As Stevie stomped past the two of them, Phil looked up in surprise. Or was it surprise? Lisa mused. Hmmmm. She chewed thoughtfully on the end of her pencil. By spending so much time with Betsy Cavanaugh, could Phil be trying to make Stevie jealous? Lisa grinned to herself. Of course he was. He'd seen Stevie and Joe together and decided to get even.

As Lisa watched Stevie march off toward the stable, Lisa reflected that Stevie got riled up much too easily. Stevie had flown off the handle without stopping to think about what was happening. Another character defect for Lisa's journal! It made Stevie seem so human. Mr. Haegle was going to love it.

In the van the riders told knock-knock jokes. And when they ran out of knock-knock jokes, they told Horse Remorse riddles.

These were Stevie's favorite, since the answer to a Horse Remorse riddle was always a rhyme, and she prided herself on being especially clever at making them up.

"What's a horse's favorite kind of party?" she called to the other riders.

They thought for a second, then Polly Giacomin said, "We give up."

"A stall ball!" Stevie cried gleefully.

When the riders ran out of riddles, they began to
sing the Horse-o-Phone song.

"Hey, Patch," started Carole.

"Is someone calling my name?" came the group's
reply.

"Hey, Patch."

"I think I heard it again."

"You're wanted on the Horse-o-Phone."

"If it isn't *Starlight*, I'm not at home."

By the time they got to the unloading spot, Red
O'Malley said that he was now deaf for life, which was
a good thing because he wouldn't have to hear them
sing anymore.

Unloading the horses seemed to take even longer
than it had to load them. And then the horses had to
be saddled. Finally everyone was mounted and it was
time to start up the beautiful mountain trails.

A cheer went up from the riders, which caused Max
to hold up his hand. "If you're eager to go, think of
how restless the horses feel. Be sure you've got them
under control."

They rode through woods, past mountain laurel and
ferns that were just beginning to open. Before long
the trail began to climb.

Carole could feel the air become cooler and cleaner
with a wonderful piney perfume. Last year Horse Wise

had camped at a meadow halfway up the mountain, but this time they were going all the way to the top of the mountain to High Meadow. They took one quick break—lunch alongside a brook—and then continued on their way.

When the riders reached High Meadow, Max halted them.

"High Meadow is absolutely pristine," Max stated quietly, "it's an undisturbed part of these mountains. Let's make sure we leave it that way."

Lisa nodded vigorously. With its silvery grass swaying in the wind, and wide, expansive view, High Meadow was a beautiful place. She was sure that when the riders weren't around, all sorts of wildlife visited this place, and she didn't want to do anything to interfere with that.

"And now," Max went on, "it's time to unsaddle the horses and set up camp."

A few of the riders groaned. It was frustrating to be in such a great spot for riding and not be able to ride. But everyone knew Max was right. There were hours and hours of work to do, and the horses had already had a long day.

The riders unsaddled the horses and put them in a temporary paddock at one end of High Meadow. Then they put blankets on the horses because it got cold at night up there. They set up camp, gathered firewood, and cooked dinner.

Finally it was time to relax. Everyone sat around the campfire with their feet toward the flames.

Carole, eager to continue with her Big Sister/Little Sister project, turned to Amie and Jackie. "What makes a horse pine?" she asked.

"Wanting to be an oak?" Amie said. She and Jackie gave each other high fives at this piece of wit.

"Not exactly," Carole said, frowning slightly. "Do you know what pining is?"

The girls shook their heads, their eyes big in the firelight.

"A horse hangs her head. Her eyes get dull. She doesn't want to eat. Sometimes she'll stop eating altogether."

"No!" Amie said. "Horses are always eating. Like Jackie."

Jackie gave Amie a violent nudge, and the two of them went over backward, giggling.

"Let's get serious," Carole said. "Horses pine when they're alone. That's why you should never have just one horse. What's a horse's most basic instinct?"

"To go back to the barn?" Amie asked.

Carole shook her head. "A horse's basic instinct is . . ."

Lisa, sitting a few feet away, could tell that Carole was not going to give a definition, but a speech. In fact, Carole was probably going to trace the development of horse instinct over the last sixty million years. Everything she'd say would be one hundred percent accurate, but the little girls only needed a little bit of information. And, knowing Carole, she would take sixty million years to do it. Lisa was beginning to feel sorry for Amie and Jackie.

"Time for Horse Charades," Max said from the other side of the fire. "Horse Wise members, take your places." He gestured to the clearing between the tents and the fire.

Jackie and Amie bolted upright, looking at Max with bright eyes. "Wait a second," Carole said. "We're not finished." Amie and Jackie drooped back down to their spots around the fire. Lisa could tell that Carole was beginning to seem less like a big sister to them and more like a big bore. Lisa stood up and walked over to them. "What makes Horse Wise riders pine?"

Amie and Jackie looked at her as if she were yet another bore. But when Lisa said, "Missing Horse Charades," they laughed.

"Yeah," Jackie said. "I'll never eat again."

"Wow," Lisa said. "That must mean you'll really be miserable if you miss the game."

41

"And I'll hang my head all day," Amie said, hanging her head.

Carole gave Lisa a grumpy look, but then she nodded and said, "Go ahead," and the girls shot off before she could change her mind.

Carole stood up and looked down at her riding boots. With the toe of one boot she flicked a crumb of mud off the other boot. Carole's boots were comfortably worn. Veronica diAngelo might worry about whether her boots were spotless, but not Carole.

Lisa made a mental note of this. Carole fussed with her boots when she was angry. It was amazing how much more Lisa was noticing now that she was keeping a journal.

Stevie joined them.

"It's the Horse Charades genius," Lisa said, looking up at her. "I bet you and Phil are planning to knock them dead."

Stevie tossed her head. "Not exactly," she muttered angrily. "This time Phil's on his own."

Gradually all the Horse Wise members gathered around Max. "Six members to a team," Max called out. "Team captains will be Joe Novick and Betsy Cavanaugh. Captains, pick your players."

With a big smile, Joe made his first choice—Stevie. Now it was Betsy's turn, and she picked Phil. As

Stevie watched, he grinned and sauntered over to sit down next to Betsy. Stevie fumed. Betsy had been flirting with Phil the whole trip, and he clearly didn't mind one bit.

When Phil glanced over in Stevie's direction, she avoided his eyes. She and he had always been competitive with one another—it was something that had caused problems between them in the past. Around him she'd learned to check this side of her personality, or at least joke about it so the two of them could laugh; but right now Stevie couldn't care less about ticking off Phil. In fact, she reasoned, making him angry would make the game even more fun.

Joe's next choice was Carole, which normally would have pleased Stevie, but today she was disappointed. Carole knew a lot about horses, but she tended to space out during games. Maybe we can still get Lisa, Stevie consoled herself. With her brains Lisa was a real asset. But after consulting with Phil, Betsy picked Lisa next, and Joe made things worse by choosing Liam, who was cute, but too young to be a real contributor. Betsy picked Veronica. Joe picked Polly.

By the time the teams were made up, Stevie knew that Joe's team was definitely the weaker one. "We'll have to try hard," she told him.

"We've got a great team," Joe said confidently. "We'll clobber them."

Max said, "The first category is book titles."

Joe and Betsy flipped a coin to see who would go first. Joe won and elected to start, so Max gave him a slip of paper with a book title written on it. Joe read it and then handed it back to Max.

Joe held up one finger to indicate first word and put his hand over his eyes and looked around.

"Search?" Stevie said. "Hunt? Pursue? Seek?"

Joe shook his head and made the same motion again. Stevie groaned in frustration. If they hadn't gotten his clue the first time, how would they be able to get it the second?

"Lookout?" Carole said. At least she was trying.

"Try another clue," Stevie urged.

Max frowned. "Team members are only allowed to guess solutions, not give directions," he said. "You're risking disqualification."

Joe pounded his heart with his fist and spread his arms.

"True love," Amie yelled.

Joe put his hands in his pockets and pretended to look for something, and all at once Stevie had an inspiration. "Miss," she yelled. "Little Miss Muffet. Mississippi." Of course, these were not book titles, and they didn't have anything to do with horses, but Joe was nodding wildly, so she knew she was on the right track.

"Miss . . ."

"Time," Max said. "Now the other team is entitled to try." He gave the answer to Betsy Cavanaugh, who read it and gave it back to him. With a big grin Betsy nodded and crooked her little finger, pretending to drink from a cup.

"Cup," Veronica said. "Dainty."

Betsy shook her head and pretended to dunk something in the imaginary cup.

"Tea!" Phil said.

Betsy nodded and then pointed at Joe's team to show that Phil should say the word they got.

"Miss," Phil said. "Tea."

Betsy made a putting-together gesture.

"Miss-tea. Misty," Phil said. "*Misty of Chincoteague.*"

Betsy gave a whoop and fell into his arms.

"Hey, charades is fun." Phil grinned.

"Especially when you have a genius on your team," said Betsy, smiling at him.

"Give me a break," Stevie muttered. Carole's eyes widened, but she didn't say anything.

"Next round will be movie titles," Max said. "The

title does not necessarily have a horse in it, but there are horses in the movie. Losing team goes first."

"I'll do it," Stevie said to Joe.

Max gave Stevie a slip that said *Treasure of the Sierra Madre*, one of her favorite movies. The only thing was, how could she pantomime the title?

She indicated that she was starting with the first word. Then she pretended to dig a hole in the ground and pointed at the hole.

"Boulder?" Joe said. "Dirt?"

She shook her head and pretended to open a box and then marvel at its contents.

"Lunch box," Amie said. Stevie knew that Amie was only six, but Amie's answer annoyed her because the team was getting further and further away from the true answer. Stevie looked at Carole. This was one of her and Colonel Hanson's favorite movies, but Carole's eyes had that blank, dreamy look they got when she was thinking about horses.

Stevie pretended she was carrying something in both hands. Then she unloaded imaginary things from it, which were supposed to be teacups, and held up the thing itself, which was supposed to be a tray.

"Platter?" Joe said.

"Shelf?" Amie said.

"Time," Max said.

46

Stevie sat down and folded her arms around her knees.

Phil took over for the other team. Stevie could hardly bear to hear Phil act out the title—the worst part was that he did exactly what she had done. He pretended to dig for something and pointed at the ground.

"Gold?" Betsy said.

Phil waggled his fingers to show that she should keep on trying.

"Silver," she said. "Oil."

Phil pointed at the trees.

"Tree," Betsy said.

"I've got it," Veronica said. "Treasure!"

Stevie buried her face in her arms. If a moron like Veronica could get "treasure," why couldn't Joe?

Phil spread his hands to show that Betsy should expand on treasure.

"Treasure Island?"

Phil shook his head and there was silence. For one moment Stevie thought he was stuck, but then he indicated fourth word and began sketching waves with his hand.

"Waves," Betsy said.

Phil grinned to show she was on the right track.

"Ocean. Water. Sea."

47

Phil nodded and then sniffed and pointed at the space beyond his nose.

"Odor. Smell. Stink."

"Air," Betsy yelled. "Sea air. Treasure Sea Air. Treasure Sea Air." She frowned, stuck.

"*Treasure of the Sierra Madre,*" Veronica shouted.

"Yes!" Phil said, leaping toward her. He and Veronica and Betsy put their arms around each other, with Peter and Jackie hanging on to their waists, jumping up and down.

A disgusting sight. Stevie turned to Carole, who had come back to life when the name of the movie was mentioned. "That's one of my favorites," Carole said. "My dad's, too."

"No kidding," Stevie said bitterly. "I guess you were too busy to watch my clues."

"I watched them," Carole said. "I just didn't understand them."

It continued downhill from there. Betsy's team won the TV-series title and the comic-book title. The only charade that Stevie's team got was for a movie star, Skye Ransom, whom The Saddle Club had taught to ride.

"The results are four for the Cavanaugh team and one for the Novick team," Max said.

Betsy's team went wild with applause.

48

Max raised his hands. "It's late. Younger Horse Wise members go to their tents and turn in. Older riders, please bank the fire and check the horses." He turned to Stevie. "You're in charge of the horses. Get someone to go to the paddock with you."

Stevie involuntarily glanced toward Phil, hoping he'd volunteer. She was still angry at him, but she realized she missed him, too. So far the MTO was nothing like she'd imagined.

But Phil was already busy laying logs on top of the smoking fire. "They'll burn all night," he said. "Hickory lasts forever. Someone pass me some pine cones."

As a rule there was no way Betsy would sully herself by picking up pine cones, but now she went over to the neat pile of logs and kindling that the riders had made earlier and scooped up an armload of cones. She carried them over to the fire and said, "Is this what you want?"

"Yeah, great," Phil said, taking the pine cones from her arms. "They'll start the logs burning." Artfully, Phil tucked cones into the spaces between logs.

There was a plume of smoke, and then the cones burst into blue and purple flames.

"It's gorgeous," Betsy breathed.

Phil smiled down on her upturned face. "Thanks."

Before she even knew what she was doing, Stevie

had grabbed the rest of the pine cones and kindling. "You think that's gorgeous, get a load of this." She threw her arms wide open, scattering pine cones and kindling into the fire.

There was a shocked silence as the pine cones and kindling caught flame. Suddenly the fire was dangerously large.

"Everybody back," Max said in a grim voice. All the riders except Stevie retreated until they were standing in the dark.

Max turned to her. "Younger riders come on overnights so they can learn from older riders," he said in a low tone. "I guess you decided to show them how *not* to behave."

"I . . . ," Stevie began. But then her words got stuck. How could she possibly explain why she'd done what she'd done?

"Yes?"

"I'm sorry," she mumbled finally.

By this time the flames had receded and the fire looked under control. The flare-up had lasted less than a minute. Stevie looked at it, relieved. "I'll go get some more kindling," she offered. After all, they were camping out at the edge of a pine forest. There wasn't exactly a shortage of pine cones.

"Not in the dark," Max said. "Go check on the horses and then turn in."

Stevie walked toward the paddock, feeling as though she'd just been sent to her room. The last thing she saw before she left the campfire had been Betsy grinning with satisfaction.

"Hey," came a voice from behind her. "Wait up."

For a moment Stevie thought it was Phil—and that he'd come after her to say he was sorry. But it was Joe.

"Need some help?" he asked.

"Yeah. I guess so," she replied reluctantly. Actually, she just wanted to be alone to drown in her own sorrows.

Joe seemed to sense this.

"Are you okay?"

"Fine," Stevie said. "Great."

"It's a beautiful night," Joe said.

Despite her bad mood, Stevie couldn't deny it. Overhead the stars seemed especially bright, and the moon was rising from behind the trees.

"Will you tell me what to do?" Joe said. "I've never inspected horses at night before. What do you look for?"

"You feel their backs to see if they're hot," Stevie said. "And you run your hands down their legs to see if they're sore. And then you go eyeball to eyeball with them to make sure their eyes are clear."

"Got it," Joe said.

When the two riders reached the temporary paddock, the horses raised their heads to look at them. In the slanting moonlight the horses seemed to have tiny heads, and legs as thick as tree trunks.

"You go left, I'll go right," Stevie said.

The first horse to greet her was Topside, the beautiful Thoroughbred that Stevie always rode. He butted her with his nose. She put her arms around his neck and buried her face in his mane. She had been looking forward to this MTO so much. And now it was so dismal.

"Topside," she whispered to him. "Why is everything coming out so different from what I expected?"

But Topside didn't answer. He went back to pulling at the silvery grass with his teeth. Stevie felt his back, which was cool, and pulled his head up so she could look into his eyes. Then she ran her hands down his legs. He seemed fine. She patted him gently. "Night, boy," she murmured.

Next she moved on to Starlight, Carole's horse. "Starlight in the moonlight," she said to him. "Starlight, star bright."

52

Starlight snorted. He seemed to think she was being silly.

She checked Comanche and Garnet. In the moonlight Garnet looked even sleeker than during the day. Her dark brown eyes looked at Stevie soulfully. "Just think," Stevie said to her, "you're going to have to spend the whole day tomorrow with Veronica, you poor horse."

"Take a look at that moon." It was Joe, who was only a few feet away.

"Beautiful," she said, looking at the silvery disk of the moon and at the hazy circle surrounding it.

"You know what they say?" Joe asked. "Ring around the moon, rain coming soon."

Fifteen minutes later, when Stevie finally got to her tent, she was not only still grumpy, she was exhausted. As she pushed the tent flap back, she saw that Carole was sound asleep and Lisa was bent over her journal.

Lisa looked up as Stevie entered. "Everything okay?" she whispered.

"Fabulous," Stevie muttered as she took off her riding clothes and put on her pajamas. "Fantastic. Glorious." She crawled into her sleeping bag and pulled it over her head. Now she knew what MTO stood for—Most Terrible Overnight.

5

"Excuse me." A loud voice cut abruptly into Carole's dream. "This is not my favorite way to wake up."

Carole opened her eyes to the light of morning. Stevie was sitting up in her sleeping bag, rubbing the side of her head. "Ouch," Stevie said.

"Sorry," Carole mumbled. She rubbed her eyes. "I was having this bad dream about giant mosquitoes."

"Well, you must have squashed every single one of them," Stevie said. "You hit me harder than any of my brothers ever have!"

At that Carole giggled. "I must have really walloped you, then."

She stretched and listened to the rain outside

pounding their tent. The air felt chilly and damp. Did this mean they wouldn't be able to ride today? Carole hoped not.

She wiggled out of her sleeping bag, then stood to pull on her jeans. Stevie was surveying her critically.

"Frankly, Carole, I think this is going to be a bad hair day for you. You look like Wanda the Witch."

Carole grinned. "Well, thank you for that boost of confidence. But may I remind you that according to Veronica, *I'm* not the one who needs the beauty makeover." She ducked as Stevie chucked a wadded-up T-shirt at her.

When Carole was fully dressed, she pulled back the flap of the tent and peered outside. "I'd better check on Jackie and Amie," she said. "Has it been raining long?"

"I don't know," Stevie said. "I was sleeping soundly until this giant mosquito hunter attacked me."

They both glanced over at Lisa, who was lying in her sleeping bag. She was wide awake and staring at them with bright, watchful eyes like a cat.

"When did it start raining, Lisa?" Stevie asked.

Lisa shrugged. "I haven't been paying attention," she said. "I've been thinking."

Stevie raised her eyebrows but didn't say anything.

If Lisa wanted to tell them what she'd been thinking, she would have done so. Stevie didn't want to pry.

When Carole left to check on the younger girls, Stevie rolled her sleeping bag to keep out the dampness. She couldn't help remembering how Phil had rolled up Betsy's bag yesterday and how foolishly Stevie had acted last night. What's the matter with me anyway? she wondered. She decided that as soon as she saw Phil this morning, she'd apologize, and they could start to enjoy themselves together on the MTO.

"I guess you never want to use that sleeping bag again," Lisa said.

"Huh?"

"You'll never be able to untie those knots."

Stevie looked down. It was true. She had tied several tight knots. She would definitely have a problem with them later. But that was later, this was now.

Outside the rain was really coming down now. We'll need rain gear for today's trail ride, Stevie decided. That is, if we can still go.

Stevie went over to her knapsack and rummaged in it, looking for rain gear. She found her hooded rain jacket and her boots. But she seemed to have forgotten her rain pants. She could visualize the rain pants perfectly. They were green, the same color as her jacket, and, she recalled with a sigh, they were lying

56

on her bed at home. Great! Her *bed* would stay dry all day.

"I forgot my rain pants," she said.

"You can use my extra pair," Lisa said. Her duffel bag was gigantic. The day before, everyone had joked that Lisa must be starting off on a really long trip—like to Mars, but it wasn't Lisa's fault. Her mother never let Lisa go anywhere without a month's supply of clothes.

"You have extra rain pants?" Stevie said, looking at the blue rain pants Lisa was holding out to her.

Lisa nodded.

"Your mother thought maybe you would grow an extra set of legs?"

"You never know."

The two of them collapsed into giggles at this, and Stevie thought that it was good to know that even in the middle of the worst rainstorm of the century, The Saddle Club still had a sense of humor.

When they lifted the tent flap, they saw that the rain was even worse than it sounded. It was coming down in long diagonal sheets. The stream that ran along the side of the clearing had disappeared, because now everything was a stream. The new spring grass was squashed.

Red O'Malley came over and suggested that they make a fire.

"In this?" Stevie said, staring at the rain.

"There's a dry spot," Red said, pointing to a spot that was sheltered from the rain by an overhanging rock.

"But the firewood we gathered must be wet," Stevie said.

Red grinned and shook his head. "The minute the rain started, I moved it into my tent." He lifted the flap of his tent to show the wood neatly stacked against the back. "Go ahead," he said. "You can build a great fire."

Stevie groaned. "There's only one problem. We don't have any kindling."

She turned to look at the pine forest. It was filled with fallen branches and pine cones. There was lots and lots of kindling. Unfortunately, it was soaking wet.

Veronica joined them. "Too bad you burned all those pine cones, Stevie," she said in a nasty tone. "What are we going to do now?"

For once Stevie didn't know what to say to her.

When Carole got to Amie and Jackie's tent, she raised the flap. The two girls were huddled inside, still in their pajamas, looking cold and scared. She had offered to keep them company last night, but they had indignantly refused, saying they weren't babies. Now they looked like miserable, damp kittens.

"Hey, guys," Carole said, giving them a smile. "Let's get things organized. No more of this lazing around."

The girls jumped up eagerly and started pulling out their clothes and rain gear. They looked happy that someone had come to rescue them.

Half an hour later all the MTO riders were standing under an oak tree with water running down their hoods, off their shoulders, down their legs.

"Sorry, guys," Stevie said. "No fire this morning."

"My fingers are cold," Amie said.

"My teeth are cold," Jackie said.

"My boots are full of water," Liam said.

Max said, "No Morning Madness for breakfast this morning." He passed out containers of orange juice and milk. Then he opened a box of granola bars. "Everyone take three and put two in your pocket—a dry pocket—for later."

A damp granola bar, Stevie thought. Just what everyone wants for breakfast. She started toward Phil to explain that she hadn't meant this to happen. But before she could get to him, Betsy appeared at his side and said, "I think this is kind of exciting."

"Wet feet are truly exciting," Phil said, but he was grinning. He raised his granola bar to Betsy as if he were making a toast.

Max turned to Red O'Malley. "It's evident that there won't be any riding today. Why don't you drive the younger riders into town this morning. I think some hot chocolate is in order."

"Yes!" Amie and Jackie gave each other high fives.

"Experienced riders over here," Max said. Seven bedraggled riders walked over to a spot next to the giant pine. "The trails have turned to creeks," he told them.

"How are the horses?" Carole asked. Stevie chuckled, in spite of the situation with Phil. It was just like Carole to think of the horses. In fact Stevie was surprised she hadn't checked on them first thing this morning before heading to Amie and Jackie's tent.

"They're fine," Max replied. "Phil and Joe helped me place rain sheets over their blankets, and none of them has stiffened. But we can't ride them until the rain stops."

"Great," Veronica said. "So we stay here and watch it drip." Stevie noticed that Veronica had a hooded raincoat with a monogram on the pocket and matching rain boots. Her black hair was shining and neat. Veronica would be well groomed even in a tornado.

"You can do that," Max said. "Or you can go for a walk. If you head back to the road and walk south half a mile, you'll pick up the Appalachian Trail. There's a six-mile walk to Hawks' Roost, the highest point on the mountain."

"Great, so we'll get a better view of the rain." Veronica sniffed. "I think I'll pass."

Max shrugged. "It's up to you."

"I'll stay at the campsite, too," Lisa said. Carole and Stevie looked at her in surprise. Lisa loved adventure. And she loved being with other Saddle Club members. "I'll just hang out," she said.

Only five riders—Phil, Betsy, Carole, Stevie, and Joe—decided to take the walk. As they set off from camp toward the road, Phil took the lead because he had visited Silverado State Forest before and knew the trails.

"It's an excellent path," he said. "You won't have any trouble with it if you watch your step."

"I love rain," Betsy said. "It makes me feel sad. You know, like *triste*. That's the French word for 'sad,' except it means more than sad. It means romantically sad." She looked in Phil's direction.

Stevie kicked a rock, which bounced off a tree. She wished she knew the French word for "bimbo."

Joe Novick watched the rock ricochet; then he glanced at her. "You okay, Stevie?"

"Terrific," she muttered.

As they walked along the trail, Stevie noticed that the dirt was covered with tiny new leaves that had been torn off the trees by the rain. Stevie leaned over and picked one up. It was the size of her thumbnail. Thanks to the storm, it would never get any bigger. There's something *triste* about that, she mused, then giggled out loud. At least she still had her sense of humor.

The center of the trail had turned into a brook, so they had to walk with one foot on either side of the water. This proved tricky because the earth was slick. As she negotiated one particularly wide spot along the trail, Stevie lost her footing. Instinctively she threw her arms out, reaching for the person who was directly in front of her.

Joe Novick turned to catch her, and for a second or two the two of them slithered sideways with their arms around each other. Finally Stevie managed to regain her balance. Quickly she disentangled herself from Joe. "Thanks," she said. "Now I see why Max was worried about the horses on these trails. They're really slippery."

The other riders had stopped to wait for the two of them.

"You okay?" Carole called out.

"Yup," Stevie answered. She glanced at Phil, expecting him to be concerned, too. But instead he looked annoyed.

"Ready?" he asked impatiently.

Stevie nodded, feeling hurt all over again, and the five of them stumbled on through the rain. Beside the path pale-pink mountain laurel petals lay scattered on the wet ground.

They passed a stand of brush that was all shades of purple from dark to lavender. "Those are blackberries," Phil called back over his shoulder. "They look nice, but look out for the thorns."

He led them into the yard of an abandoned farm. The house had vanished, leaving only a stone foundation and a scrolled metal gate. But the barn was still there, and in good condition with a second-story overhang. Phil stood under it and called back to the rest of them. "Come on and take a breather. There's a steep climb ahead."

Betsy scooted in next to him, and Carole and Joe lined up next to them. Stevie stood apart from the others, watching the rain pound the old wrought-iron gate. If the conditions weren't so bad, she'd be tempted to turn back to camp. But there was another piece of her that didn't want to be defeated so easily. She'd been waiting to go to this MTO for a whole year—was she really going to let Phil and Betsy ruin it for her?

As it turned out, Phil hadn't been kidding about the climb. When they started out again, the path turned stony and rose steeply over slippery rocks. Stevie, being last, walked in a shower of pebbles.

The campers climbed hard, grasping branches along the incline. Then suddenly the sky was bright. It hadn't stopped raining, but there was an odd silver light.

Phil was standing on a lookout carved into a rock. To Stevie's surprise he gestured for her to join him. As she got close, Stevie couldn't help but notice how green Phil's eyes were and how his hair was black with rain.

"Look at that," he said, pointing toward the west where Stevie could see the dim shapes of mountains. "There's good weather over there."

"How do you know?"

"There's light shining through thin patches in the clouds."

"Wow," Stevie said. "You can read the weather."

Phil looked at her. Was he thinking what she was

thinking? she wondered. Was he wishing they were alone together?

"It's soooo romantic," said Betsy, popping up between them.

"Yeah," Stevie muttered. "It's totally *triste*."

LISA HAD DECIDED to stay behind at the campsite because she had so much to enter in her journal. She was especially eager to capture the way Stevie had reacted to the game of charades and the way Carole was handling Amie and Jackie.

Mr. Haegle had told Lisa to write two hundred fifty words a day. But two hundred fifty words weren't nearly enough, she decided. She was in the middle of her third page when Max stuck his head into the tent.

Max looked worried. "The horses are getting restless," he said. "Especially Teddy. It looks like he might spook the others. Can you come and help?"

Lisa stood up. She knew what Max meant. When horses got panicky, they were almost impossible to control. They could buck and run or even jump a fence and take off. It was a real danger, because a spooked horse could easily injure herself or her rider.

Anything could happen during weather like this. Max needed her help. Lisa tossed the diary aside and reached for her rain gear.

CAROLE'S LESSON FOR Amie and Jackie was that horses are herd animals—if they aren't with their companions, they pine and sometimes even die. Meanwhile, as Carole was going on about this, Jackie and Amie were sneaking looks at the other riders around the campfire, longing to join them. Carole noticed that Jackie and Amie weren't paying attention, so what did she do? She told them to stop fooling around.

If Amie and Jackie had been horses, Carole would have noticed immediately that they wanted to be with their friends. Since they were human, she missed it entirely.

The same thing happened this morning. Carole informed Jackie and Amie that in a way they were lucky it

66

was raining. That way they'd have more time to learn about horses. The only thing that saved them was when Max announced that Red O'Malley was taking the younger riders to town for hot chocolate.

Stevie chuckled. No question but that Lisa had Carole's number.

When Stevie had come into the tent a few minutes earlier, looking for a dry sweater, she had happened to notice the journal lying open on Lisa's bedroll. Stevie had also happened to see Carole's name, so of course she had to look. Now Stevie knew she should stop reading, but somehow she couldn't bring herself to put the small notebook down where it belonged.

Why is Carole so much more interested in animals than humans? I think it has something to do with the fact that she grew up on army bases and has always been moving around, having to make new friends. Horses have become something she can count on. And, when Carole's mother died of cancer, horses became even more important to her. They're like her refuge. Sometimes I think Carole needs to pay a little more attention to humans. The Saddle Club understands her, but not everyone else does!

It's been interesting to observe Stevie, too.

Stevie wiggled down onto the bedroll for extra comfort. This was going to be interesting.

*Last night Stevie was so determined to win Horse Cha-
rades that she messed up the clues and turned Joe Novick
into a nervous wreck.*

Stevie looked up. This wasn't true. Their lousy
team's losing had been entirely Joe's fault.

Stevie read on.

*And then when Betsy told Phil that his fire was
goooooorgeous, Stevie completely flew off the handle and
threw all the kindling in the fire.*

Stevie looked up. Lisa's English teacher was going
to think that Stevie was the biggest idiot on earth.
Members of The Saddle Club were supposed to stick
with each other through thick and thin, not criticize
each other. Lisa might have a point or two here, but
how could she say these things about someone who
was supposed to be her best friend?

Suddenly it felt as if the journal were burning a
hole in Stevie's lap. She wanted to throw it on the
floor. Better yet, she wanted to throw it out in the
rain, where it would dissolve and disappear forever.

But then Lisa would know that she had read it.
Stevie figured she might as well know the rest of the
bad news, so she picked it up and started reading
again.

It's fine to be competitive. That's one of the things that makes Stevie such a great rider. But last night Stevie got carried away. She let her competitiveness cause even more trouble with Phil.

Stevie felt her face burn. Who did Lisa think she was?

Just then there was a sound outside the tent. Stevie caught her breath. It must be Lisa. She didn't want Lisa to know that she had read the journal. Never. No way. She put it where she found it.

When Carole came in, her hair was stuck to her forehead and her nose was shiny. "It's bad out there," she said. "The horses are getting spooky. It's not that they couldn't handle the rain at first, but there's been so much. They feel like it's never going to end."

Stevie yawned. "Rain always makes me sleepy. I thought I'd come in here and take a rest."

"Really?" Carole said, looking at her with surprise. "With all that noise?" Carole glanced at the bedroll where Stevie was sitting, noticed that it was Lisa's, and wondered what was going on.

"So what is Max going to do?" Stevie said quickly.

"He's going to move the horses into the forest," Carole said. "It's safer there. The only problem is that it isn't going to be easy to move them. They're on the edge of panic."

Carole took off her boots and then her socks. Underneath, her feet looked pale and wrinkled. She rubbed them. "The dampness really gets to you."

"You can say that again."

Carole looked at her. "Are you okay? I mean, is there something wrong? You look a little funny."

"No," Stevie said. "I'm great. No problem. Feeling excellent, as a matter of fact. I'd better go help with the horses."

Stevie put on a dry sweater and then pulled her rain jacket over it, tightening the drawstring of the hood. Outside, the oak tree was black with rain, and the grass had disappeared under a sheet of mud.

Stevie took a deep breath and pushed her way through the rain.

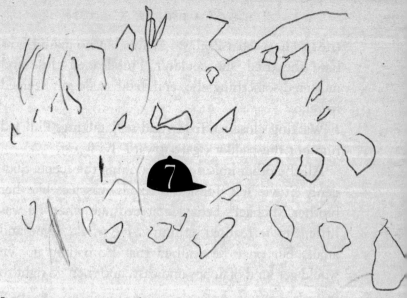

7

LISA HAD TRIED everything, but nothing had worked. Teddy was getting more and more edgy, and she could feel from the tension in his neck and legs that he was about to take off.

Suddenly Phil and the other hikers appeared from the edge of the forest.

"Phil," Lisa said. "Help! I'm so glad to see you. The horses are getting skittish, and we have to move them under forest cover, but Teddy won't budge."

Phil came over and took Teddy's halter and put his arm around his neck and whispered something in his ear. Teddy snorted, but listened.

Stevie, holding Topside a couple of yards away,

tried to hear what Phil was saying, but no matter how hard she tried, she couldn't. Phil leaned close and muttered something else, and Teddy suddenly seemed to relax.

Walking close to Teddy and still talking, Phil led him out the paddock gate toward the forest.

All the other horses were watching the scene. Suddenly Stevie felt Topside relax. It was just like her brother Michael's behavior at bedtime when he was little, Stevie realized, grinning. He would argue and argue, but once he realized that he had to go, he would get kind of floppy and easy, and then go right to bed.

Stevie and Topside walked through the gate after Phil and Teddy, with the other riders and horses following. Phil led them into the hemlock forest, where it was dark and cool.

"Thanks, Phil," Max said, leading Garnet into the group of horses. "We're lucky to have you on the overnight."

"I'm enjoying it," Phil said. "I'm learning a lot." He looked pointedly at Stevie.

What does he mean by that? she wondered.

"The last thing you want to do is let horses panic in a storm," Max said to the riders. "When they run in

72

fear, they can hurt themselves, especially when it's slippery."

There was a quiet moment while everyone thought of what would have happened if the horses had bolted from the paddock.

"Look," Phil said.

There was a glint of sun overhead, one sunbeam, as clear and sharp as an icicle.

"Oh," Amie said.

The sunbeam shivered and split until it was a cluster of rays reaching through the trees.

"It's like being inside a Christmas tree," Amie said.

What a perfect image, Lisa thought, as everyone stood watching the sunlight spread over them.

"Back to the meadow," Max said. "The horses will be glad to see the sunlight, too."

They had a reverse parade then, walking out of the woods, into the wet grass at the edge of the meadow. Because of the rain, the grass was full of colors: purple stems, rusty leaves, bristly white seeds.

As soon as they reached the meadow, Topside and Garnet began to grab the grass with their teeth.

"Pull the horses' heads up," Max reminded the riders. "They can get colic from eating wet grass."

Stevie knew this was true. She'd once seen a horse with colic. The horse's stomach was as tight as a drum, and its muscles were swollen. If a horse wasn't treated promptly for colic, it could die.

"Keep them moving," Max said. They walked the horses to the high point of the meadow, a knoll with a stand of rust and yellow flowers called Indian paintbrush.

"Look," Phil said.

Stevie reflected, with irritation, that Phil was always telling people to look. But then, when she saw what he was referring to, her annoyance melted away. On the other side of the valley was the beginning of a rainbow. It traveled to the center of the sky.

"Where does it end?" Jackie asked.

Phil winked. "Look for where it ends," he said. "Remember, there's a pot of gold at the end of every rainbow."

Amie and Jackie traced the rainbow's path with their eyes. Miraculously it seemed to end at the cluster of Indian paintbrush.

The two girls immediately charged over, but when they arrived, the end of the arc was gone. Laughing, they darted from spot to spot. The other riders looked on, amused.

Lisa came over to Stevie and said, "We'd better go back to camp and get the grooming kit to dry the horses."

"Says who?" Stevie demanded. Why was Lisa telling her what to do? How come she always knew best? "Get it yourself."

Lisa's jaw dropped. "The horses shouldn't stand around when they're wet," she said. "You know that; they'll cramp."

Stevie glared at Lisa. This was great. First Lisa had criticized her personality, and now she was questioning Stevie's horse knowledge. Lisa was saying that Stevie didn't even know how to take care of her horse.

"I think I can take care of Topside myself," Stevie said. "Thank you very much."

Lisa wondered what in the world could be wrong with Stevie. Why was she suddenly on her high horse? Lisa noticed that Phil, who had heard what Stevie said, was looking at Stevie with confusion, too.

"Forget it," Lisa said. "I'll get the grooming kit myself."

"You just do that," Stevie snapped.

Lisa turned away. If Stevie didn't want to go with her, maybe Carole would. Carole was climbing the hill toward the paddock, looking thoughtful. It was odd that it had taken Carole so long to get dry socks —she'd left the paddock twenty minutes ago, knowing that Max needed her help with Starlight and the other horses. Carole was spacey sometimes—but not when it came to a horse in need. Something must be up.

"Stay right there," Lisa called down the hill to Carole. "We'll go back to camp and get the grooming kit."

But Carole didn't seem to hear her. She continued up the hill, her eyes cloudy.

Jackie and Amie saw Carole and ran toward her. "We saw a rainbow," Jackie said. "We didn't find the pot of gold, but we're still looking. Want to help us?"

"Maybe," Carole said without much interest.

"It's the biggest rainbow ever," Jackie said. "So the pot of gold is bound to be the biggest ever."

"We'll be millionaires," Amie said.

"Actually, gazillionaires," Jackie said.

"Trillionaires," Amie said.

"That's stupid," Jackie said. "Everyone knows that a gazillion is more than a trillion."

Amie slipped her arm around Carole's waist, and Jackie held on to her left arm. "How come horses get scared from rain?" Jackie asked.

Carole was about to explain that lightning and falling branches were dangerous to horses, so they were right to be scared. But then she remembered Lisa's journal. The last thing that Amie and Jackie wanted was another boring horse lecture.

"I guess they're afraid their coats will shrink," she joked.

Amie's face fell. "Horses' coats don't shrink, Carole. That's not true."

Lisa was surprised. She'd never heard Carole answer a question about horses in this manner. "What happened to our professor of horse-ology?" she asked. "The answer should take you at least a week."

Carole gave her a grumpy look. "You think so? Would a week be enough for me and my big mouth?"

Lisa drew back, wondering what had gotten into Carole. Maybe the storm had spooked her, too. Or maybe it was the fact that they'd spent the whole morning not riding. That was it: Carole loved horses so much she got grumpy when she couldn't ride.

Just then Phil walked over to them. "What's going on here, guys? The horses need to be rubbed down."

"I'm on my way to get the grooming kit," Lisa responded. She looked at Carole again. "Want to come with me?"

But Carole just turned away. "Why don't you get it yourself?" she muttered.

Phil and Lisa looked at each other. It seemed as if half of The Saddle Club had gone crazy.

8

"TOPSIDE DOESN'T SMELL like a wet horse anymore," Stevie said. "*I* smell like a wet horse." The riders were in the paddock rubbing down the horses. The horses had been blanketed and covered with rain sheets during the storm, but their heads and necks and legs were wet.

Carole took a sniff of Stevie, and it was true. Stevie had the ripe, steamy smell of a soaked horse. "Phew," Carole said. "Don't go to a dance smelling like that."

"No problem there," Stevie said, grimly thinking of Phil and Betsy. "No one will ever ask me."

Max came over to see how they were doing, and Stevie noticed that he was pretty grubby himself. It seemed as if the dirt and damp had moved from the horses directly to the riders.

"Horses dry?" Max said.

"They are, but we aren't," said Carole.

Max grinned. "Now that the horses are clean, it's time to clean the riders. Go back to your tents and change clothes and come back. I've got a surprise for you."

With relief Carole and Stevie went back to the tent to put on clean clothes.

When they returned to the meadow, the other riders were dressed in dry clothes, too.

"The trails are too wet to ride," Max said, "but the meadow isn't. I've tested it myself and the footing is fine. So saddle up for horse games."

A cheer went up from the riders because horse games were almost as much fun as a trail ride.

"We'll start with Maximillian Mandates," Max said. "Here are the rules. When I give an order, follow it if I say 'Maximillian mandates,' but ignore it if I don't." He looked at the younger riders. "Do you understand?"

"Sure," Amie said.

"It's just like Simon Says, only on horseback!" Jackie exclaimed.

"Exactly." Max beamed at her. "First we'll play a practice round. All riders circle left."

"That's easy," Amie said, putting a gentle pressure on her horse's left rein and pressing him with her right knee. Her horse moved in a tight circle.

"Hoooooo," Jackie said. "Maximillian didn't mandate."

Under her hat Amie's face turned red. "I knew that," she said. "I was just fooling."

"Oh, sure," Jackie said, and Amie's face turned even redder.

"That was only a practice round," Max reminded them. "Now Maximillian Mandates begins in earnest. Maximillian mandates all horses move sideways to the left."

Horses hate to move sideways because to a horse there's just no point in moving to the side. To a horse ahead is the only way to go. So all the way down the line there was arguing and maneuvering between horses and riders. Finally all horses had moved to the left.

"Maximillian mandates all horses make a figure eight."

This was easy. It was something even the younger riders could do. Within seconds all the horses had completed figure eights and were back to their starting spots.

"Excellent," Max said. "Take four steps forward."

Veronica diAngelo, who had probably been thinking about her perfect fingernails, Stevie decided, shook the reins and let Garnet take four steps forward.

"Maximillian didn't mandate," Amie yelled.

"So?" Veronica sniffed. "Who cares?"

"You're out of the game, Veronica," Max said. "Move to the sidelines."

Veronica rode Garnet to the edge of the field.

"Maximillian mandates four steps to the rear," Max said.

Horses dislike walking backward even more than they hate moving sideways, so there was a lot of persuading of horses, but finally all the horses moved back.

"Who can be first to gallop around the rocks?" Max said, pointing to a group of rocks that looked like sheep feeding in the grass.

Phil's horse Teddy took off toward the rocks. Phil hadn't signaled him to do that—Stevie could tell from the look of annoyance on Phil's face—but four other horses followed.

The only riders left now were Stevie, Lisa, and Carole, plus Amie, Jackie, and Peter Allman.

"Show me how good your communication is with your horse," Max said. "Get your horse to canter without using your reins or your heels."

"Easy," Amie said, and she was off with Jackie and Peter after her.

But Maximillian hadn't mandated, so they were out of the game.

Now there was no one left but the three girls in The Saddle Club. Lisa looked at Carole and Stevie. Usually the three of them would be having fun. But today Carole and Stevie were acting cold and unfriendly.

"Maximillian mandates do the Piaffe," Max said.

This was one of the hardest of all movements. It meant that the horse had to trot in one place. If horses hate to move sideways, or backward, they really hate trotting without getting anywhere.

Carole had recently been working on the Piaffe, so she walked Starlight, then urged him into a trot, and then slowed him to the Piaffe, making it look easy.

"Max may mandate, but can I do it?" Stevie muttered to herself. Topside could do the Piaffe because he was a show horse. The problem wasn't Topside; it was Stevie's timing, knowing when to give him the command. Stevie moved Topside into a trot and then slowed him. Topside was almost there, but then he couldn't stand the frustration and jumped forward.

Stevie was out of the game.

When Lisa tried to slow Comanche into a Piaffe, he tossed his head, as if to say that she must be kidding, and came to an abrupt halt. The game was over.

"Carole wins," Max said, "and by the way, Carole, that was an excellent Piaffe."

Carole's cheeks were glowing.

The next game was Horse Professor. Every time someone answered a question about horses correctly, the rider and his or her horse got to take a giant step forward.

"Can we place bets on the winner?" Phil grinned. "Because if we can, I'm betting on Carole."

"That's right." Amie nodded vigorously. "Carole is the best."

"Why bother to compete?" Veronica said. "It's not worth the trouble."

"Wrong!" Max said. "Carole is not going to be the winner, because she is going to ask the questions."

A groan went up from the riders. "We'll be here all night answering Carole's stupid questions," Veronica muttered. "Frankly, I'm not into it." She turned Garnet away from the other riders.

"That's fine," Max said evenly. "Good luck to the rest of you riders."

The riders lined up facing Carole and Starlight. Carole gritted her teeth. This was not exactly the job she wanted, but she didn't want to let Max down. "Okay," she began, "why do foals graze with their knees bent?"

"So they can moonwalk," Stevie said, and everyone giggled.

"Very funny," Max remarked. "Does anybody know the real reason?"

"To wear out their knee socks," Betsy said.

"Brilliant." Carole looked around. "Does anybody really know?"

Amie jumped up in her saddle and raised her hand. "I know. I know."

"Why?" Carole said.

"Because their legs are so long, their heads can't reach the grass."

"That's right," Carole said. "Take a giant step. Now, how long does it take a horse to digest an apple?"

"What kind of a question is that?" Betsy said.

"I know," Polly Giacomin said. "It takes a day. Because an apple a day keeps the horse vet away."

Carole shook her head. What was the point of this?

No one was taking her seriously. They all thought she was a bore.

"You're out of the game, Polly," Max said. "And the next person to make a joke is out of the horse games altogether."

Great! Carole thought. I'm such a loser that Max has to stick up for me. She looked at him, hoping he would end this game, but he nodded and said, "Continue."

"How long does it really take?" she said.

"It takes a horse four days to digest anything," Jackie said.

"Excellent. Take a step forward."

Phil and Amie and Jackie kept getting the right answers until the three of them were neck and neck.

"Final question," Carole said. "How do you know when a horse is totally miserable?"

Phil was still thinking about it when Amie and Jackie raised their hands and bounced in their saddles, yelling, "Me! Me!"

"Both," Carole said.

"When the horse is pining," the girls said together.

"It's a tie," Max declared. "And I think we can see here that not only is Carole a true professor of horse-ology, but also a great teacher."

Ha, Carole thought. Here's a good Horse Professor

question—who can make horses seem dull? Carole
Hanson.

Next came the relay race. Max made Stevie head of
one team and Veronica head of the other. Veronica
picked Phil, and then Stevie picked Carole. Veronica
picked Joe Novick. Next Stevie picked Lisa. She was
still angry with her friend, but there was no way
Stevie could let Lisa get stuck on Veronica's team.
Lisa flashed Stevie a small smile as she signaled Comanche to move to that side of the field.

By the end of the picking, Veronica had nothing
but boys on her team with the exception of herself
and Betsy Cavanaugh.

"I guess Veronica thinks girls can't ride," Stevie
said to her team. She said nothing about the fact that
Betsy and Phil were on the same team again.

"Let's show her," Carole said.

"These will be your relay batons," Max said, hand-
ing a stick to Stevie and one to Veronica. "Here's the
course. You go around the stand of Indian paintbrush." He pointed to the bristly orange and yellow
flowers. "Around those pale-gray rocks that look like
sheep, and then around the mountain laurel." He
pointed to the bushes with pale-pink flowers. "And
then back. Ride fast, but not too fast." He looked at
the younger riders, Amie, Jackie, Peter, and Liam.

"Anyone who loses a stirrup or a rein will have to start over again."

Stevie named Carole to ride the first lap and Lisa the second.

Lisa noticed that Stevie didn't look at her when she made the assignment. Great, Lisa thought, she may have picked me, but she's not about to talk to me.

Stevie named Amie and Jackie to ride the next laps. Lisa noticed that she looked at *them*. And then Polly Giacomin, and finally Stevie herself, riding the cleanup lap.

"Riders ready. Start," Max said.

Carole and Starlight burst away from the group, cantering easily through the wiry meadow grass, making it look like fun, a sign that the horse and Carole were in perfect communication. Veronica on Garnet was not far behind, but Garnet was wasting energy, using too short a stride. Veronica wasn't riding him properly.

Starlight floated around the Indian paintbrush and toward the rocks, while Veronica, riding too low over Garnet's neck, urged her on. A good rider, like Carole, showed confidence in her horse. She didn't push. Veronica, on the other hand, was overeager. She was pushing Garnet too hard, throwing her off her stride.

By the time Carole and Starlight got to the rocks,

they were a length ahead. By the time they got to the mountain laurel, they were ahead by a length and a half.

Carole handed off the stick perfectly, so by the time Lisa got to the Indian paintbrush she was two lengths ahead.

"Now, listen," Stevie said to Jackie and Amie. "We have perfect position. All you have to do is not ride too hard. Did you see Veronica?" The girls nodded. "Don't push your horse. Help him concentrate, but don't force him, because he wants to win even more than you do."

Lisa handed off to Amie, who took off, her eyes shining.

"Amie!" Stevie called. "Not so fast."

Amie's excitement had passed itself to her horse, and the two of them were barreling toward the rocks.

"Heels down," Stevie yelled. But it was too late. One of Amie's feet had slipped through the stirrup.

"Stop your horse," Max called. "Rider back."

Amie brought her horse to a jolting stop, regained her stirrup, and headed back. By the time she got back to Max, Liam, who was on the other team, was rounding the rocks. Amie had lost the lead and then some.

Amie's face was streaked with tears. "I wrecked it," she said. "I blew the race."

Stevie glanced over at the other team. Betsy was hanging on to Phil's shoulder, anxiously biting her nails as she watched Liam head back. "Come on, Liam," Betsy shouted.

Stevie looked back at Amie. Stevie really wanted to win this relay, but the words in Lisa's journal came flooding back to her: *It's fine to be competitive . . . but last night Stevie got carried away. . . .*

"Nothing's wrecked," Stevie said firmly to Amie. "Trust your horse."

Amie rode out again, her back straight, head tall.

Liam came cantering in and passed off to Peter. By this time the other team was four horse lengths ahead. There was no way Stevie's team could catch up, short of a miracle. Polly Giacomin rode better than Stevie had expected and picked up half a length, but by the time Stevie set off on the final lap, she was three and a half lengths behind Phil. It doesn't matter who wins, she told herself. The important thing is to be a good sport and have a good time.

Looking ahead, she saw that Teddy wasn't cantering well. He was digging his feet too deep and springing too high. Teddy was losing ground. This was the opportunity Stevie's team needed, and Stevie was determined not to let it go by.

She leaned over Topside's neck and said, "Go."

Topside flew over the grass toward the Indian paint-brush. Stevie steered Topside wide, not wanting to get in Teddy's way.

Teddy was almost prancing—not something a horse should do in a race. Phil was leaning low over his neck, talking to him. Phil must have said something right, because as Stevie drew even, Teddy began to canter again with Phil crouched low in the saddle.

Stevie leaned closer to Topside's neck, and the horse's stride lengthened. His gait was so smooth that Stevie could scarcely feel the hoofbeats. She was part of his motion. Tears were streaming out of the corners of her eyes and her throat was dry from the wind.

When she and Phil approached the finish line, they were neck and neck. At the last second Topside made a huge effort and managed to cross the line a whisker ahead. "Yes!" shrieked Stevie. She put her arms up, making victory signs with both hands. Her teammates gathered around her, yelling, "We won! We won!"

When Stevie turned around, she saw Phil sitting on Teddy, watching her. Her face colored. I did it again, she realized. All I thought about was winning—and beating Phil. Lisa's right. I have absolutely no self-control.

But Phil rode over to her and said, "Nice race."

"You mean it?" she said, filled with relief.

"Sure." Phil looked at Topside's chest, which was flecked with foam. "We'd better cool them down."

"I'd say it's a must." Stevie grinned.

They rode together toward the trees. Teddy was still prancing nervously.

"I'm sorry Teddy was spooked," Stevie said. "It wasn't fair."

Phil looked at her, his green eyes shining. "A race is a race. Whatever happens is fair. You raced well. That's what counts."

Stevie felt a wave of relief. It was practically the first time Phil and she had spoken since they left Pine Hollow. Now at least some of the tension had broken.

Phil reached down and ran his hand along Teddy's neck. "Teddy has this thing about weather and loud noises. On the Fourth of July when firecrackers and rockets go off, he stays in his stall waiting for the world to end."

"Poor guy," Stevie said. "What do you do to calm him? As a matter of fact, what did you do out there during the race? You said something to him."

Phil smiled. "One of these days I'll tell you. I'm just waiting for the right moment."

"So what's wrong with now?" Stevie said, turning to him with a smile.

But a voice called to them from the top of the

meadow. Stevie and Phil turned in their saddles. It was Carole, motioning them back to the group. "Time for the postmortem," she called. Reluctantly Stevie turned her horse around, and Phil did the same.

"Good racing," Max said when they returned. "I hope you all learned something from that." He looked at all the other riders, but especially at Amie and Veronica. "A horse wants to win a race. What you as a rider have to do is help your horse stay calm and concentrated. You have to help your horse run his own race."

Tears gathered in Amie's eyes again.

But then Max added, "Even more important is to keep on trying. Horses are just like people—they make mistakes sometimes. As a rider you have to let your horse know that one mistake isn't the end of the world. And that's what Amie did."

Amie grinned.

"And now, what I suggest," Max said, "is that some of the riders get the horses ready for the night, and the others start a fire." Max looked at the sky, which was turning pink in the west. "I predict a clear, cold night with lots of stars. We'll need a good fire so we can stay up and tell horse stories."

"Horse *ghost* stories," Stevie clarified. "I feel one

coming on already. It's about this ghost rider in the sky who's in this Ghostly Ghastly Relay Race."

"Later," Max said with a grin. "First the fire. Stevie and Phil, you two can make it."

"You're on." Stevie quickly slid down from Topside and handed the reins to Jackie. As Phil dismounted, Betsy approached him.

"That was great," she breathed. "You handled Teddy so well. I was afraid you were going to be thrown. It was masterful."

Somehow Betsy has managed to come between us again, Stevie thought furiously. She was staring at the back of Betsy's head with its shining chestnut hair, every strand in place.

"Thanks," Phil said. "There was a minute there I thought I was going to wind up in a tree."

"Not you," Betsy said. *"You* would never wind up in a tree."

Is he going to help me, or flirt with her all day? Stevie thought. In disgust she looked away from Betsy and glanced at Phil's horse, Teddy.

As if he were reading Stevie's mind, Phil spoke up. "Hey, Stevie, let me give Teddy to Liam, and we'll get started gathering firewood."

Stevie frowned. Now she was watching Teddy closely. The horse was shaking his head and pawing the ground. "Maybe you should stay with Teddy, Phil. He's still acting restless."

At that moment Max came up. He looked concerned. "That's right," he said. "If you want a good ride tomorrow, it's worth spending time with him tonight, Phil. If he has a bad night, he'll be impossible to ride in the morning, and I'm counting on you to help supervise the trail ride."

Phil looked disappointed, but he could hardly argue with Max. "Okay. Sure."

"Stevie, why don't you ask Carole for help?" Max said.

Stevie looked over at Carole, who was holding Starlight's reins. "Do you want to come and gather firewood and start the fire?"

"Sure," she replied. She gave Starlight's reins to Max and looked around. "Seems to me we could use a couple of expert assistants."

Carole went over to Amie and Jackie and said, "How would you like to help Stevie and me gather firewood and start a fire?"

Amie looked toward the woods. "I don't know," she said. Then she and Jackie exchanged glances. It was clear they didn't want to go.

"It'll be fun," Carole promised. "We'll talk."

Amie and Jackie looked at each other again. Then

Jackie said, "That's okay. I think we better stay here and help."

Carole's face fell. Stevie, watching her, could tell that Carole felt terrible. Amie and Jackie had such a good time during the horse games that Carole must have thought that all her problems with them had disappeared. Now here they were, unenthusiastic about her again.

"Come on," Stevie said, touching Carole's arm. "We don't want to wait too long. It's getting dark."

"Sure," Carole said, turning to her. "We better do that. We wouldn't want to eat cold hot dogs."

"You forget how much work overnights are," Stevie said as they headed toward the woods. "All the things you take for granted at home, like heat and light, you have to provide for yourself out here."

"I don't mind that," Carole said. "I just wish Amie and Jackie were having fun."

CAROLE AND STEVIE walked into a pine grove. The dried-up needles crunched under their boots.

"There's one good thing about this overnight," Stevie said.

"There is?" Carole said. "Tell me about it."

"I got to see that Phil is madly in love with Betsy Cavanaugh."

"No, he's not," Carole stated. "He thinks she's a total drip."

"So that's why he spends all his time with her."

"You mean that's why he spends all his time *running away* from her."

Stevie shrugged. "I don't know what's going on between him and me. But I'll tell you one thing I do know. I have to stop acting so competitive around him. It's like I just get carried away or something."

Carole blinked. Stevie's words sounded just like Lisa's journal. She glanced at Stevie. Was it possible that Stevie had read Lisa's journal, too? She wanted to ask her, but then again, if Stevie hadn't snooped, Carole didn't want to offend her.

"Listen," she said finally. "There's no point in getting upset about being upset." She stopped, trying to put her thoughts together. "What am I trying to say?"

"That I should lighten up?" Stevie said.

Carole giggled. "I couldn't have put it better myself."

Stevie stopped and picked up a pine cone. "I guess we could use a few of these."

"Good idea," Carole said.

Stevie filled her arms with pine cones, and then Carole piled small fallen branches from pine trees on top. "We can't gather the good stuff like hickory, because it will still be wet," Carole said as they walked deeper into the forest. "We'll have to go for the fast-burners like spruce and ash."

"How do you know that?" Stevie asked.

Carole grinned. "Just another boring bit of MTO lore."

They found a white ash tree that had fallen on top of an old log so that it wasn't resting on the ground. "I believe we're in luck here," Carole said. She inspected the broken end of the tree. "It's still dry."

Stevie stood on top of the ash tree and jumped on it to break it in half. But when she landed, there was a dull thump and then nothing more. "This is one tough tree," she said, and jumped again.

This time when she landed the trunk rocked, tossing her off into a drift of soggy leaves. "Great," she said, getting up and picking up the pine cones and kindling she'd dropped. "I think I need your help. How about lending some of the weight of all that horse knowledge of yours to the job of breaking this trunk?"

"No problem." Carole giggled and climbed up next to Stevie.

When the two of them jumped, there was a cracking sound. They climbed off and bent the two halves of the trunk toward each other, breaking them.

"Two more jumps and we're out of here," Stevie said.

When the two girls headed back to camp, the sun was low in the sky.

"I guess you saw what happened with Amie and Jackie," Carole said. "They didn't want to come and gather wood. They're tired of my horse lectures." She sighed. "Sometimes I think I'm better around horses than people."

Hmmmm, Stevie thought. There was something familiar about this. Could it be that Carole had read Lisa's journal, too? Should she ask Carole and find out? But then Stevie realized that if Carole hadn't read the journal, she'd just be making trouble between her and Lisa.

"Amie and Jackie are tired," Stevie said. "They're little kids, and it's been a big day for them—an immense day when you come right down to it."

Carole shrugged. "I guess I wanted to teach them everything—for instance, I thought they'd want to know that a horse won't eat toadstools in the woods."

Stevie shook her head. "Believe it or not, Carole, they've had enough of horses for today."

Carole turned to Stevie. "That's the reason? And I thought it was just because they think I'm a big bore."

Stevie giggled. "Well, I wouldn't put it exactly that way, but if you insist . . ."

At that Carole burst out laughing. One of the wonderful things about Stevie was that she could often help Carole to see the humorous side of things—even if it had to do with Carole's own worst side. She'd wanted to do a good job on the Big Sister/Little Sister project and she'd just gotten carried away. Carole had to admit that Lisa had said pretty much the same thing about her in her journal. Only there it hadn't been funny. It had hurt.

Stevie and Carole came out of the woods onto the edge of the meadow, where the tips of the grass were pink with sunset light.

"The meadow really changes," Stevie commented.

"What?"

"It's different every time you look at it."

From the other side of the hill came voices and laughter.

When Stevie and Carole reached the top, they could see the campsite and the temporary paddock. The horses had been unsaddled and groomed, and now they were standing lazily, flicking their tails to keep away flies. The younger kids were running around the campsite, playing some kind of tag. The older riders were bustling with preparations for dinner. It was almost like watching a family.

Carole and Stevie walked slowly down the hill. When they reached camp, Max looked at their logs and said, "Nice work. White ash is a good bet for dryness."

The two of them made a ring of stones and laid a bed of twigs and small branches inside. They put four logs on top and lit the kindling with a box of matches that had been protected from the damp by being dipped in paraffin. The twigs sputtered and smoked, sending off a toasty smell, and then the logs suddenly caught fire.

"Am I glad to see that," Joe Novick said. "I felt like I was going to be damp for the rest of my life."

The riders gathered around the fire and watched it flare and take hold.

"Ten more minutes until I make my special hot dogs," Phil said. "These are known as Phil's Phabulous hot dogs. 'Phabulous' with a *ph,* of course."

"That's too long to wait," Amie said.

"I'm practically dead with hunger," Jackie said.

"They're worth waiting for," Phil promised. "You haven't experienced phabulous until you've had one of my hot dogs."

"I *know* it," came Betsy's voice. "I can't wait."

Carole and Stevie looked at each other, and Carole pressed her lips together as a sign that Stevie should let it go. Stevie went over to where Joe and some of the others were wrapping potatoes in aluminum foil.

"That was a great race you ran," Joe said.

"Thanks," Stevie said.

"You really know how to handle your horse."

"Thanks, Joe," Stevie said. "You too."

101

The riders finished wrapping the potatoes and brought them over to the fire. They tucked them against the inside of the ring of stones. Soon the stones would be as hot as the fire, so the potatoes would be baked from both directions.

"Take a look at this," Phil said. He had used two long, skinny branches to spear fourteen hot dogs. He held the hot dogs over the fire and said to Amie and Jackie, who were watching him, "The secret is to crisp them without burning them."

"Crisp yes, burn no," sang Amie.

"Brisp no, curn yes," sang Jackie.

Phil had positioned the hot dogs exactly the right distance from the flames, so they sizzled without catching fire. At exactly the right moment Phil turned them over to crisp the other side. Then, when they were done, he said, "My assistant will now do the buns."

He had been looking at Amie, but Betsy pushed her way forward and grabbed the buns. "The secret is to toast, not burn," Betsy said.

Stevie wouldn't have believed it, but Betsy managed to do it without scorching a single bun. Then Betsy slid the hot dogs into the buns.

Stevie usually didn't like hot dogs—and she was hoping to hate this one—but actually it was delicious, especially when it was slathered with lots of mustard. She finished her first one, and then she was still so hungry, she had a second. Probably she would wake up in the middle of the night with a severe case of hot-dog breath, but she didn't care.

Phil tested a baked potato with a fork and pronounced it done, so he fished the rest out with the fork and distributed them. Stevie's potato had a slightly smoky flavor with a distinct woodsy tang. But both of these tastes were completely eradicated when she added sour cream, cheese, sauerkraut, pickles, and onions. It wasn't just on ice-cream sundaes that Stevie liked to eat weird combinations.

At last they all lay back with their feet to the fire. This was the first hot meal that they'd had since they started on the MTO.

Stevie looked up. The stars were so bright, they seemed to be hanging just behind the trees, and the air was so clean, it smelled sweet. Out in the forest there were foxes and raccoon and deer, maybe even a bear or two. Here around the fire it was safe and warm.

Someone started to sing, "Home, Home on the Range." Amie and Jackie—and Peter and Liam, as well—sang in high soprano voices. A deeper voice rumbled off-key. Stevie looked—it was Red O'Malley.

And then a clear, strong voice rose through the other voices, ". . . seldom is heard a discouraging word, and the skies are not cloudy all day." It was Phil.

Betsy Cavanaugh was sitting next to him, her hair shining in the firelight.

Stevie looked back up at the stars. Tears formed in her eyes. It seemed like days since they'd left Pine Hollow for the Mountain Trail Overnight. Back then she'd thought it would be a special time for her and Phil. Now she was wondering if the two of them would ever even be friends again.

10

When Lisa woke, there was a terrible racket. She rolled over in her sleeping bag and wondered why the younger kids were making so much noise at this hour. But then she realized it wasn't a *human* racket; it was birds. She slipped out of her sleeping bag and got dressed as noiselessly as she could, but Carole opened her eyes and looked at her.

"Birds," Lisa said. "It sounds like they're starting a riot."

Carole started to work her way out of her sleeping bag, but Lisa couldn't wait. She had to see what was going on.

There were two blue jays with bright eyes picking

at crumbs around the campfire. In the dark last night Lisa hadn't realized that Horse Wise members were such messy eaters. Another blue jay fluttered down to the spot where Amie and Jackie had been sitting. The blue jay grabbed a piece of hot-dog bun and tried to fly with it, but the bun was too heavy, so his tail flew skyward while his beak remained stuck in the bun.

The blue jay came back to earth and took small hops, banging the bun along the ground until a piece tore off, and then he flew over the hilltop with his prize.

Max came out of his tent, yawning. "Birds like a balanced diet," Max said. "A worm, a bun. Maybe a little mustard."

It was a perfect morning, bright and warm. At last, Carole thought, we're going to have a really long ride.

"Everybody eat quickly," Max said. "We've got a busy day ahead. Carole, you rouse the younger riders; I'll wake the older ones."

In twenty minutes everyone, even Veronica di-Angelo, was dressed and ready to go. There was no time to have Max's Morning Madness, including his famous Maxerino; instead they had granola bars and fruit.

After breakfast Max held a brief Horse Wise meeting. "This is going to be a great day," he said. "But we'll have to ride hard if we want to meet the vans on time on Tuesday. The trail is dry in spots, but not in others. We need to know where we can canter and trot and where it's still not safe, so we need scouts."

He looked at Stevie. "You did so well as the fox on the mock fox hunt last fall, I'm going to make you one of the scouts." He turned to Phil. "I'm going to make you the other scout because you know Silverado State Park. I want the two of you to ride a mile or so ahead, check the trail, see where we can make up for lost time and where it's dangerous. We'll wait until you come back and give us a report."

Sounds perfect, Stevie thought bitterly. Max must have designed this day especially to torture me. Last night had been no fun sitting around the campfire listening to Phil croon to Betsy Cavanaugh, but at least she hadn't been alone with him. Stevie opened her mouth, about to give some kind of excuse, such as that she wasn't really awake, but one look at Max told her that he was worried. Stevie knew that he needed an exact report on trail conditions. Suddenly, being a scout for Max seemed like too important a job to let her petty differences with Phil get in the way.

Stevie and Phil saddled their horses in silence and mounted them in silence. Teddy was edgy, the way he'd been last night. But again Phil managed to soothe him until he was calm.

They rode around the edge of the meadow to where the trail entered the wood. "How about it?" Phil asked.

"What?"

He nodded at the trail ahead, which was flat and looked dry. "Let's trot."

"Sure," she said. "Why not?"

Ahead of her Teddy broke into a trot. Stevie pressed Topside with her knees, and he began to trot smoothly, head up, glad for the action. The rain had flooded away a great deal of dirt, so the rocks on the trail were loose and exposed. As they trotted, there was a shower of pebbles.

"Rocks," Stevie called.

Phil reined in Teddy, who didn't like it. The horse pranced and tossed his head, making a snorting, complaining sound. Phil turned in his saddle. "It's bad ground."

"Too many rocks," Stevie agreed. "We might have to stop and pick the horses' hooves every ten minutes."

Phil got a funny look. "I guess you and Joe Novick could take care of that." Then he turned, and at the top of the hill, where there was another flat stretch, he put Teddy into a trot and then into a canter.

Stevie felt stunned as she gave Topside the signal to trot after Teddy. Was Phil actually jealous of Joe Novick? If so, he was completely wrong about how Stevie felt. But it certainly did explain a lot. Maybe that was why Phil had let Betsy Cavanaugh follow him around, Stevie mused.

"Hey, the thing about Joe Novick . . . ," Stevie called as she cantered after Phil, but he didn't seem to want to stop and listen.

They came around a bend in the trail. There was a fine clear trail ahead under oak trees. As Phil leaned forward, Teddy cantered faster. Topside stretched his neck, lengthening his stride. Ahead Phil let Teddy go flat out, his hooves sending back plumes of dust into Topside's and Stevie's faces. The riders thundered alongside a blueberry patch and past a stand of skunk weed.

Then Phil slowed Teddy. There was a gravelly creek bed ahead. He guided his horse onto the mossy edge of the trail where there were no stones, and then through the clear creek water.

"The thing about Joe . . . ," Stevie tried again.

But Phil and Teddy were off, trotting past a gathering of ferns and crossing a field. Phil was definitely trying to avoid her.

"All I wanted to say," she yelled, "was—" But at this instant Teddy broke into a canter. Stevie could hear his hooves thud on the brown winter grass.

Abruptly there was a flash of white ahead. A fawn darted across the road in front of Teddy, its tail high.

Without warning Teddy reared, giving a whinny that sounded to Stevie like a scream. The horse's front legs frantically pawed the air as the small deer disappeared into the woods as swiftly as she'd emerged. Phil's arms were around Teddy's neck, his knees high. Then, as Stevie watched in horror, Teddy lost his balance and fell with a thud. Phil flew off the horse and landed in the rocks beside the trail in an awkward position. Terrified, Teddy scrambled to his feet and turned and galloped past Stevie, his reins flapping.

Stevie had halted Topside when she spotted the deer. Now she jumped out of the saddle, tied Topside to a tree, and ran over to Phil. His face was pale and his eyes were closed.

"Phil? Phil? Are you okay?" There was no answer.

But when she leaned close, she could feel his breath on her ear. She told herself she had to be calm because Phil needed her. She remembered Max saying that you should never move an unconscious fallen

110

rider. You should wait for help. Teddy would probably gallop back to camp, where Max was waiting with the other riders, and Max would come and look for them.

Stevie knew she shouldn't move Phil, but she couldn't bear the sight of his head lying on the rocks. She sat next to him and gently lifted his head into her lap.

The black fabric on his helmet was torn, and under the tear she could see a dent. If Phil hadn't been wearing a helmet, he might be dead. Tears filled Stevie's eyes. Oh please, Max, she prayed silently, hurry!

Stevie took Phil's hand. It was terrible to feel how limp it was. She shivered. Maybe if she talked to him, it would help somehow. "You never let me tell you about Joe," she began softly. "I mean, I don't care about Joe. It's you I care about." Stevie swallowed. "This whole trip I thought you liked Betsy Cavanaugh. Maybe you do, I don't know. But the thing is, I like you. All week I was thinking about coming here with you." She closed her eyes, remembering how she'd imagined taking a special bareback ride alone with Phil on the MTO. "We were going to ride bareback at dawn," she went on. "Kind of stupid, huh? We were going to ride out in the dawn, and then we were going to—"

"Make out?"

Stevie jumped and her eyes popped open. Phil's eyes were open, and a trace of color had returned to his face. Slowly a grin appeared on his face, and Stevie had the feeling he'd heard every word she'd said. In fact, he must have let her think he was knocked out.

He smiled at Stevie's astonished expression.

"How . . . ?" she started to say, but she was so filled with relief and surprise that the words wouldn't come.

And that was fine with Phil. He reached up, put his hand behind her head and drew her down closer. Stevie closed her eyes and then . . .

Topside neighed.

There was a clattering of hooves and Max appeared on the trail, leading Teddy by the reins.

"No harm done, I see," Max said with a twinkle in his eyes.

Phil sat up. "Is Teddy okay?"

"He's fine," Max said. "A little shook up, but okay."

"It was a fawn," Stevie hastily explained. "Otherwise Teddy was doing great. He wasn't spooked at all. But then this fawn came streaking out of the woods and he reared. Phil flew off his back."

At that Max looked concerned. He tied Teddy to a nearby tree and approached Phil. Quickly he checked Phil for injuries. "Nothing's broken," he said finally. "Are you up to riding?"

"No problem," Phil said as he stood up. "In fact, you would have to hire an army to keep me off the trail today."

Max grinned. "That's the kind of spirit I like to see in a rider. Come on, we'll meet the others."

Phil got back up on Teddy. Stevie mounted Topside and they headed back, riding side by side behind Max.

Phil grinned at her. "Too bad we were rescued so soon."

11

BACK AT CAMP Max consulted his two scouts, Stevie and Phil, and decided that the trails were sufficiently clear and dry for all the riders to manage.

Eagerly the members of Horse Wise mounted and set out. It was a crisp, cool spring day, and the sky above the canopy of trees was bright blue. There would be no rain today.

On the trail the riders galloped alongside a rushing stream. They jumped an old stone fence. At lunchtime they ate in an old apple orchard, and at sunset they cantered across a meadow that seemed as if it would never end. Lisa noticed that this time Phil and

Stevie rode close to one another the whole time. Obviously, the two of them had patched things up.

Shortly after dinner Lisa headed for her tent. It had been a great day of riding, and now she was exhausted. She'd certainly enjoyed the mountain trail, but it would have been a lot more fun if Stevie and Carole had been more friendly. The two of them were still barely speaking to her, and Lisa didn't have a clue as to what was going on. Maybe she'd have a chance to talk with them tonight.

Lisa undressed quickly and crawled into her sleeping bag. She had one more thing to do before she could sleep—write in her journal. She pulled out her notebook and pen and then reached into her duffel for her flashlight. Carefully she rested the light on top of her sleeping bag so she could see the journal better.

Then Lisa noticed that the pages looked slightly grubby. Lisa was always neat—it was something she couldn't help—in her house everyone and everything was neat. When she was little, she had a gerbil, and even the gerbil was neat. She was the only kid she ever knew who had a neat gerbil.

So how come she had a slightly grubby journal?

She turned the pages. There was a crinkle on one corner. Lisa didn't crinkle corners.

But she knew someone who did. In her mind's eye

Lisa saw the math paper that Stevie once wrote analyzing the baby-sitting and housecleaning service she ran briefly. Every corner was crinkled.

Trying not to panic, Lisa flicked back to the part she had written about Stevie and reread her description of Stevie's competitiveness with Phil. This was fine for Mr. Haegle to read, but not fine for Stevie. Lisa closed her eyes. Now she knew why Stevie had been so cold and aloof for the past two days. She had been hurt.

And then Lisa thought of Carole and the way she'd been acting, too. No question Carole had also read the diary. Lisa felt like a total loser. She'd hurt two of the people she loved most in the world.

Lisa sighed. She loved writing. She loved it almost as much as being in The Saddle Club, but it seemed that every time she wrote something like the articles in *The Willow Creek Gazette* it got her into more trouble than she would have believed possible. Now she wished she'd never been assigned this stupid journal.

On the other hand, Lisa reminded herself, what were Carole and Stevie doing reading her journal? Everyone knows diaries and journals are private.

"Hey, hey, hey." Stevie popped into the tent. "Has this been a great day or what?"

It wasn't really a question; or rather, it was a Stevietype question, which demanded no answer, but Lisa heard herself responding. "I guess," she said in a flat voice.

"You had a problem with this day?" Stevie said. "Maybe you hate sunshine. And riding. And mountain trails."

"I said it was okay," Lisa said. "It was an okay day."

Carole bustled in. "There's really something wrong with MTOs."

"What?" Stevie said.

"They don't go on forever. And they make everything else look bad."

"So let's take off," Stevie said. "Let's ride around the world."

"There's all that water," Lisa said glumly.

Stevie and Carole looked at her as if they had noticed her for the first time. Then Stevie spotted the journal in Lisa's lap, and she knew exactly what was up. Lisa had figured out that Stevie had read it. Maybe this hadn't been a perfect day after all.

Carole also noticed the journal in Lisa's lap and realized what had happened right away. Lisa knew that she had read it, and she was angry and hurt, and she was right to be. Carole should never have opened it.

Carole looked down. She felt awkward and wanted

to clear the air, but she couldn't just come right out and confess, could she?

Suddenly Carole thought of Mrs. Reg, Max's mother, who ran the office at Pine Hollow Stables, and who always seemed to know what was going on. Mrs. Reg had a way of solving problems without seeming to solve them. She did it through telling stories.

Carole wasn't a great storyteller—Lisa was the writer here—but Carole knew that she was going to have to do her best.

"I'm thinking of a horse I once knew," Carole began. A lot of Mrs. Reg's stories began that way. "This horse's name was Inky on account of the fact that he was—"

"Black," Stevie jumped in, instantly catching on.

Carole nodded and continued. "He was a great horse, one of the stable's best. A new rider came to the stable and was assigned to some of the easy horses, but then one day she was given Inky. This was a real honor, and his new rider wanted to live up to Inky, but she didn't know exactly how.

"Finally she decided the best way to do it was to study the mistakes of other riders."

"I do that," Stevie said, nodding. "I think everybody does. You look at other riders and see that their hands are too low. Or they're too bossy. Or that they crowd their horse on jumps. Or that they try too hard."

"Exactly," Carole said, glad for the help. "The only thing was that Inky's rider decided to keep a record of the other rider's faults, so she kept a log. Every day, after class or Pony Club or whatever, she wrote down every mistake she saw. And all riders make mistakes."

"Even you," Stevie said.

"Yes," Carole said. "The harder you try, the more mistakes you make. Sometimes I think I make more mistakes than anyone. So there was no problem in what Inky's rider did. The only thing was that one day another rider found her log. It was poking out of her knapsack, though that was no excuse. The other rider read it and got furious. Not that the things in the log were wrong."

"It's because they were right," Stevie said. "If they hadn't been right, they wouldn't have hurt so much."

"Exactly. So that rider showed it to another rider, and pretty soon the whole stable was furious. They were in the wrong—they shouldn't have read something that was private—but they were furious anyway."

"What you're trying to say is that you read my diary," Lisa blurted out.

"Yes," Stevie admitted softly. "I can't hide it."

"Me, too," Carole said, sitting down on her bedroll.

Stevie looked at Carole. "*You* read it?"

Carole nodded.

"I thought I was the only one," Stevie said. "I mean I thought I was the only one who was a big enough rat to do that."

"No." Carole giggled. "I'm as big a rat as you."

"It was a really terrible thing to do," Lisa said. "And it's not funny."

"I wouldn't have done it," Stevie burst out, "if it hadn't been lying there. I mean, it almost seemed like you wanted me to read it."

"You figured wrong," Lisa said. "It's my personal property. Even if I'd been writing a novel that had nothing to do with you, I wouldn't want you to read it."

Stevie wrinkled her nose. "Who would write a novel on an MTO?" she said. "That would be completely nuts."

Lisa looked at her and giggled. "I don't think even I could do that."

"I'm really sorry," Carole said. "I knew I shouldn't have done it, but once I had, I was ashamed to mention it and I was angry. The worst part was, I couldn't tell you what had made me mad."

"It was terrible," Stevie agreed.

120

But Lisa wasn't completely mollified. "How would you like it if I listened in on a phone conversation you had with Phil?"

"You can't," Stevie said. "I only talk to him when I'm sitting in my closet with the door open just a crack."

Lisa grinned. "Well, I'm sorry if you two were hurt —I think you took everything the wrong way. Mr. Haegle said I was supposed to develop my characters' weaknesses as well as their strengths, so I was concentrating on making you seem vulnerable and human, like he said. You both have plenty of wonderful qualities; I just hadn't gotten around to them yet," Lisa quickly added.

"It's okay, Lisa," Carole replied. "We get it. And to tell you the truth, I learned something about myself from your journal. I was driving Amie and Jackie crazy. I guess I'm just human, that's all."

"Really, Carole?" Stevie chimed in with a serious expression. "Why, I thought you were one hundred percent horse."

At that all three members of The Saddle Club burst out laughing. At last they were friends again.

12

BY FIVE A.M. the next morning Stevie decided that she
had had enough of lying awake. She inched out of her
sleeping bag and reached for her clothes.

"You, too?" Carole whispered.

"Me three," said Lisa, poking her head out of her
sleeping bag.

They couldn't see each other because it was so dark
inside the tent. "Let's get dressed," Stevie whispered.

"What're we whispering for?" Lisa whispered.

"Because tents have ears," Carole replied.

Lisa opened the tent flap. The pine tree opposite
the tent looked like a monster with arms, but the sky
behind it had a tinge of gray light.

"We've got to get going," Carole whispered. "We're almost late. Dawn comes fast." They tiptoed toward the temporary paddock.

"What about Phil?" Stevie whispered.

"What about him?" A dark shape appeared from behind the pine tree and fell in beside her.

"Did you sleep?" she whispered.

"Yeah, perfectly . . . for about five minutes."

They passed Max's tent, and then the tent where Amie and Jackie were sleeping. There was not a sound. But as they approached the paddock, they could hear the horses tearing clumps of grass and snorting.

"They're fueling up for a great ride," Carole whispered.

They got their horses' bridles and blankets and straps from under an oak tree.

"What's that?" Stevie jumped because something had just pinged her on the head. They must have been discovered.

"An acorn," Phil said. "Acorns fall at dawn."

She beamed at him. He knows everything, she thought contentedly.

In the temporary paddock the horses were suspicious. Topside raised his head from the grass and looked at Stevie as if he had never seen her before.

Stevie was miffed at first, but then she realized that at this hour she probably looked like a large gray monster. She put her hand next to Topside's nose so he could smell her. Then she strapped the blanket onto Topside's back and slipped the bridle over his head.

The only problem with riding bareback, Stevie remembered, is mounting the horse. She looked around. Outside the temporary paddock was a large gray rock. She led Topside to the rock, climbed onto it, and then clambered onto his back.

Topside nickered. There was something special about riding bareback. Topside loved it because there was no tight girth around his belly. He had a sense of anything goes. That, as Stevie recalled, was another problem with bareback: You had to remind your horse that you are boss. Pressing with her knees, she made Topside stop dancing.

Phil mounted Teddy from the same rock and rode him in a circle back to her.

"How is he?" she asked.

"Okay," Phil said. "Totally normal."

It was funny, Stevie thought; after horses got spooked they were often extra calm for a while, as if they were trying to prove that they weren't nutcases.

"So where do you want to go?" Carole asked Stevie.

Stevie and Phil grinned at each other. "How about

the top of the meadow?" Phil said. "It should be a good place to catch that sunrise."

Walking slowly because it was still dark and the grass was wet with dew, they climbed toward the top of the meadow. "Look," Lisa said.

There were a couple of large gray birds with long scrawny necks, big shoulders, and ugly faces. "What are those?"

"Buzzards," Phil said.

"I can see why calling someone a 'buzzard' is an insult," Lisa said. "Those are the ugliest birds I ever saw."

"Not to them," Phil said. "Buzzards think they're beautiful."

They got to the edge of the meadow just as the sky turned silvery pink in the east. There was a movement to the right, nothing big, more like the movement of a leaf, but then Stevie saw that a family of deer was standing at the edge of the woods. The deer watched the horses, alert. The horses looked back, especially Teddy. But then Phil leaned over Teddy's neck and said something to him, and Teddy shook himself, as if he were shaking fear away.

They reached the spine of the meadow and rode along it to the easternmost point, where they could see a dark, deep valley, filled with hemlock trees. On

125

the other side was Hawks' Roost with its lookout point. Beyond were green mountains and sky. Behind the mountains, Stevie knew, were valleys filled with horse farms and the Silverado River. On the other side of the Silverado River was Willow Creek and home.

A flash behind Hawks' Roost and a sliver of the sun appeared. The bottoms of the clouds turned pink while the tops were still dark gray.

"There they are," Phil said to Stevie. From far down in the valley two dark shapes were rising. Stevie listened, and she could hear the faint call of hawks, high-pitched and scratchy but beautiful.

The hawks barely moved their wings, tilting themselves into the airstream, rising and circling around each other, and then flying so high their cry couldn't be heard anymore.

"They're high hawks," Lisa said. The hawks seemed to have no fear. They went higher and higher, tracing loops in front of the clouds.

"Do you think they see us?" Carole asked Phil.

"You know the expression 'eyes like a hawk'?" he said. "They can see us better than we can see them."

"I'm glad I'm not a rabbit," Carole said. "I wouldn't stand a chance!"

The sun burst out from behind Hawks' Roost across the way, sending slanting light over the horses' ears.

"How about a canter?" Phil said. "Or maybe even a gallop."

They took off over the grass. Lisa felt her legs tighten around Comanche. There were no stirrups, riding bareback, no safety; only her and the horse. If someone had told Lisa two years ago that she would be doing this—streaking through a meadow at dawn riding bareback—she'd never have believed it.

Carole on Starlight got to the end of the meadow and turned to wait. When Lisa reached her, she reined in Comanche and stopped.

"Don't look back," Carole said.

"How come?"

"Give them a second," Carole said.

Lisa realized that the sound of Stevie's and Phil's horses was getting fainter and fainter. Finally she couldn't stand it anymore and turned.

Stevie and Phil had disappeared. The meadow was empty.

"What happened?" Lisa said, thinking of how Phil had been thrown the day before. "Maybe Teddy got spooked again."

"I think Stevie and Phil are okay," Carole said with a smile. "Maybe even more than okay."

127

* * *

WHEN LISA AND Carole got back to camp, Jackie and Amie were up and furious.

"Where were you?" Amie said to Carole. "We looked everywhere."

"Everywhere twice," Jackie said. "We asked Max. He didn't know either." They looked at Carole as if they might never forgive her.

"We went to see the hawks," Carole said. "They're early risers. Birds generally are early risers. They like to hunt at dawn."

"No kidding," Jackie said. "Don't they get tired later? Do birds take naps?"

"Only when their mothers make them."

Amie and Jackie giggled, and Carole beamed back.

"If I were a bird, my mother would never catch me," Amie said. "I'd fly away to no-nap land."

"In no-nap land everyone yawns all day," Carole said. "It's kind of a drag."

"Oh," Amie said, thinking about it.

"I'm going to help with breakfast," Lisa said. "Today is the day of Max's Morning Madness. I've got to help with the Maxerinos. You think Phil's famous hot dogs were great, wait until you taste a Maxerino."

"I can't wait," Jackie said.

"It looks to me like they'll be ready in fifteen minutes," Lisa said, leaving Carole with the girls.

"Let's check on the horses," Carole said. "They may be thinking about breakfast themselves."

"So why don't we give them Maxerinos?" Amie said. "They must be tired of grass and oats and hay."

"Horses are health-food nuts," Carole said. "They don't like that stuff."

"I love horses," Amie said. "But in some ways they're kind of strange."

As they headed toward the paddock, Amie took Carole's right hand and Jackie her left. "You know something, Carole?" Amie said. "It takes a horse four days to digest an oat."

"You're kidding me," Carole said. "Where'd you ever learn an interesting fact like that?"

13

MR. HAEGLE ASKED Lisa to stay after class on Thursday. He waited until the last of the other students had drifted out of the room, and then he put his glasses on top of his head and said, "Ahem."

Lisa could see that her journal was lying on his desk.

"Have a seat, Lisa."

She sat in the chair next to his desk.

"I read your journal," he said, tapping it with his forefinger. "It's excellent. I'm impressed by your out-standing character development. Stevie and Carole really leap off the page. I feel as if I know them. And you gave them real, believable human faults. Did you enjoy the assignment?"

Lisa sat there looking at Mr. Haegle. Had she enjoyed the assignment? At first . . . but not after Carole and Stevie had found the journal. "Yes and no," she told the teacher finally. "Stevie and Carole found the journal and read it, and they both got . . . furious."

Mr. Haegle smiled. "A writer's life is full of suffering," he said. "Whoever told you it would be easy?" He pushed the journal across the desk to her. "I hope you'll continue to work on your character sketches."

Lisa picked up the journal and thanked him. As she headed out of the classroom, she thought about what he'd said. If writing is supposed to be hard, she decided, then I'm on my way to a very promising career.

THE NEXT AFTERNOON The Saddle Club met at TD's, the ice-cream parlor at the local shopping center. It was the first time they'd had a chance to get together since the MTO.

When the waitress came over, Stevie said, "I'll have raspberry ice cream with butterscotch sauce and chocolate sprinkles and a couple of maraschino cherries on top."

"That's all?" said the waitress, who was used to Stevie's strange orders. "You must be cutting back."

"You know," Stevie said, getting a dreamy look in her eyes, "I think you're right. Top it off with a scoop of bubble-gum ice cream."

"Why did I ask?" the waitress muttered as she wrote it down.

"I'll have a hot-fudge sundae," Carole said.

"Just vanilla ice cream for me," Lisa said.

"So Phil and I are going to see a horse movie on Saturday," Stevie said. "Guess what it's called."

"I'm afraid to," Carole said.

"*Night Mare on Elm Street.*"

Carole and Lisa groaned.

"I found out Phil's secret," Stevie said. "The special thing he does to soothe horses."

"What?" Carole said. Anything that had to do with horses was interesting to her.

"He talks to them," Stevie said.

Carole shook her head. "What's special about that? We all do that."

"Not in pig latin," Stevie said.

Carole and Lisa were so stunned they didn't say anything.

"You sort of put the first letter of a word at the end

and add an ay," Stevie said. *"At'sthay owhay itay orks-way."*

"If only I'd known," Carole said. "After all these years of using the reins."

"Only one problem," Lisa said.

Stevie gave her a questioning look.

"It's not pig latin, it's horse latin."

"Excellent," Stevie said. Then she looked at Lisa. "I still need to thank you for what you said about me in your journal."

"Oh, sure," Lisa said. "You're eternally grateful."

"I am," Stevie said. "I was really making a fool of myself with Phil. You made me see what I was doing."

"Me, too," Carole agreed. "I met Amie and Jackie at the stable yesterday, and we had a great time. I only mentioned fifteen facts."

"Instead of the usual fifteen hundred," Stevie chimed in with a grin.

"It's a relief," Carole said. "I can stop trying so hard. You know, I was even getting on my own nerves."

"Same with me," Stevie said. "Next time I get angry at Phil, I'm going to talk to him about it instead of doing something stupid like dumping all the kindling on the fire or getting really competitive."

Carole and Lisa looked at each other. Stevie's

words sounded good, but it didn't seem likely that self-control would ever be one of their friend's major strengths.

"Phil's secret with Teddy has helped me solve my problem with my brothers, too," Stevie told her friends.

"How?" Carole asked.

"From now on, when Phil and I talk on the phone, we'll talk in horse latin so those creeps can't understand us."

"Brilliant," Lisa said.

The waitress brought over their ice cream, and the three of them ate it in silence. Lisa was thinking how great it was that The Saddle Club was back together again. They'd had problems before, but this was their worst problem yet, because it had driven them apart.

The waitress came over and looked at Stevie's half-empty ice-cream dish. "You're actually eating that stuff."

"I may have a second serving," Stevie said. "Possibly even a third."

"I was trying to tell my family about this, but they didn't believe me," the waitress said.

"Actually, she's matured," Carole said. "She used to be much worse."

Stevie gave her a nasty look, which turned into a grin.

At last they gathered up their books and got ready to leave.

"Summer's coming," Carole said. "Think of all those great rides coming up."

"And adventures," Lisa added.

"Lots of adventures," Carole agreed.

On the sidewalk outside Stevie spotted something in the distance and turned to her friends. *"Illway ouyay ooklay atay atthay?"* she whispered. Then, in case they didn't understand her horse latin, she nodded at a couple coming toward them on the sidewalk.

It was Betsy Cavanaugh holding hands with Joe Novick.

ABOUT THE AUTHOR

BONNIE BRYANT is the author of more than sixty books for young readers, including novelizations of movie hits such as *Teenage Mutant Ninja Turtles®* and *Honey, I Blew Up the Kid*, written under her married name, B. B. Hiller.

Ms. Bryant began writing The Saddle Club in 1986. Although she had done some riding before that, she intensified her studies then and found herself learning right along with her characters Stevie, Carole, and Lisa. She claims that they are all much better riders than she is.

Ms. Bryant was born and raised in New York City. She lives in Greenwich Village with her two sons.

Saddle Up For Fun!
Join The Saddle Club

As an official Saddle Club member you'll get:

- *Saddle Club newsletter*
- *Saddle Club membership card*
- *Saddle Club bookmark*
- *and exciting updates on everything that's happening with your favorite series.*

Bantam Doubleday Dell Books for Young Readers
Saddle Club Membership Box BK
1540 Broadway
New York, NY 10036

SKYLARK

Bantam Doubleday Dell
Books for Young Readers

Name _____

Address _____

City _____ State _____ Zip _____

Age _____

Offer good while supplies last.